IN THE MIDDLE OF MANY MOUNTAINS

In the Middle of Many Mountains

Stories by

NAHAL SUZANNE JAMIR

Press 53
Winston-Salem

Press 53, LLC
PO Box 30314
Winston-Salem, NC 27130

First Edition

Cover design by Kevin Morgan Watson

Cover art, "There Used to be a Mountain," Copyright © 2013
by Alan Judge, used by permission of the artist.
www.JudgeDesign.co.uk

Printed on acid-free paper
ISBN 978-1-935708-79-7

To Lee, for his keen mind, his kindness, and his love

"A mountain keeps an echo deep inside itself.
That's how I hold your voice."

—Rumi, "Buoyancy"

Acknowledgments

The author wishes to thank the editors of the following publications where these stories first appeared.

"In the Middle of Many Mountains," *Meridian*

"Heart of a Locust," *Los Angeles Review*

"In Perfect English," *Carolina Quarterly*

"Stories My Mother Told Me," *Ruminate Magazine*

"Foundling," *2012 Press 53 Open Awards Anthology*

In the Middle of Many Mountains

Stories My Mother Told Me

A picnic and a warm day, but my mother shivers. Eating outside has never appealed to her. She removes food from the basket, and were it not for the soft earth beneath, her dissatisfaction would be heard.

My mother lives alone, and she prefers her outings to involve her grandson. She hates living alone, but since my father died two years ago, that has been her charge. And with it, loneliness and grief and frustration. Still, despite my son Faraz's absence, she is here, mainly because I asked her to be. In her old age, my mother has become more eager to please me, even though she knows I won't let her live with us. My family and I are moving to California, the other side of the country, in two weeks, and she wants to go with us.

My mother wants to take Faraz on long walks and to teach my American wife how to cook Persian dishes. My mother would tell my family her stories. But like me, my wife and son would realize the irrelevance of these stories. We are American, and we're heading west.

My mother can't even remember her own stories. Many times, I have asked her to retell a tale, and she said, "I don't remember that one. It must not have been very good." I always claimed, *It was!*

She took advantage of my enthusiasm and told me a new story, which she would later forget. Though I only heard some of my mother's stories once and only half-listened to others, they are returning now, pouring out from the recesses of my memory like they have something to prove. Stories are nonsense and disappointment—something your mother never remembers or cares about once you're grown up. It's like your life as a child was a lie. I won't let the stories out to contaminate my own son. I will rid myself of the anxiety these tales impose. Today, I will return these stories to my mother, and I'll be ready to leave her and her cautionary tales, her happily-ever-afters, her family histories, her nonsense, her failed imagination.

Okay, one hundred birds walk into a sports bar. An old man in a Hawaiian shirt sitting on a stool turns to check them out, but he's seen crazier. The bartender is bald and wears a t-shirt with sleeves ripped off. He looks like he should work in a tougher venue.

The birds rejoice because they basically have the place to themselves, except for the old man in the Hawaiian shirt. Party central. Feathers and sunflower seed shells on the floor. Toilets filled with white shit. Birds perched on stools shoved around by birds behind them trying to get a drink. Hummingbirds piss everyone off by hovering behind the bar, drinking the beer straight from the tap. All the birds laugh at the clumsy men on the televisions.

The old man in the Hawaiian shirt can hardly stand it. He tells the birds that there is a bird named Simorgh who can grant them true happiness at a bar called Qaf. *Qaf* means mountain, which is a pretty bad name for a bar. Anyway, all of the birds quiet down, turn to one another with looks of delight. Birds are generally depressive creatures, which is probably why they drink so much. The birds spend hours discussing the idea of Simorgh. One says, "He's a robot!" Another says, "No, he's the mystic Rumi." And another says, "A space child from another dimension." Finally, the old man in the Hawaiian shirt gives them directions to Qaf.

The bartender remembers money, profit, and suddenly doesn't like the idea of losing all these customers. Birds drink a lot, and they tip well. The bartender discounts all of his alcohol just as the birds are ready to leave. Needless to say, half of the birds decide to stay. To the old man's dismay, most of the birds that remain are bluebirds and titmice. The other half of the birds shake their heads or bob them up and down in disgust and head out for Qaf.

Halfway down 1st Avenue, the birds encounter a hot dog stand. Well, the sign says "Hot Dogs," but the vendor also sells hamburgers, pizza, and nachos. Nine drunk birds can't resist, so they stay to try everything on the dry-erase-board menu.

The rest of the birds hang a right onto MLK Boulevard. As they cross 2nd Avenue, they run across a Ben Franklin lying on the ground. A male redbird snatches it and declares he's going to buy a new stereo. Another male redbird doesn't think it's fair that one bird gets the money when they all found it together. So, he starts a fight. The rest of the birds sense this conflict could last a while, and they move on.

On the corner of MLK and 5th Avenue is the largest nudie bar the birds have ever seen. It's called Lavand, doves out front strutting their stuff. Nine birds are lost.

Thirty birds walk into Qaf. From the outside on 7th Avenue, it looks like a typical bar: a neon sign that reads "Qaf" followed by a little neon mountain. Inside, though, is a glorious sight. The birds are surrounded by mirrors. Not just on the walls, but on the ceiling and floor. There is a lantern in the middle of the room, and its light dances all around them. The light also reflects playfully in the mirrors. On and on. The thirty birds mill about, looking for this guy Simorgh. Even after hours, all they see are their own reflections. The birds are lost.

"No," my mother says, "that isn't right. It's filthy."

"I made it real."

"It's just like your baseball, Massoud," she says. "You want to wear it like you're proud. But it has nothing to do with you."

When I was in high school, she burned my letter jacket because she didn't want me playing baseball. She'd put up with it for so many years. But that jacket pushed her too far.

As I protested the smell of burning wool and leather, she smiled nice and wide, and her eyes wouldn't focus. She looked drunk, only she hadn't touched a drink in her entire life. An act of heroism.

My father didn't have much to say about it. He just shook his head in disgust, which was all he could do, really, not because he loved her but because my mother was what Americans call a force. I could never see through this power of my mother's, to see her love for my dad or me. Surely, she must have loved us terribly, must have sacrificed a great deal. What else justified the anger that went along with that power?

"In California," my mother says, "they are filthy. There are hippies and drugs." I laugh at her, and she smiles. Then, she says, "I have a secret to tell you about your father."

I ask her to tell me, but she says that I must wait. "Mother," I say, "you must tell me." But she refuses. She tells me to continue with my stories.

Qays and Leyli were in love. Both fathers were chieftains. Both families were well off and were respected. Yet, there were rumors about Qays being insane. One night, the townspeople said that Qays sheared a sheep and ate the wool. Leyli's father refused to have her marry Qays. She was only to see him one last time to say goodbye. Qays gave Leyli a ring and promised to love her forever. He said that he would go out in search of her and that eventually they'd be together.

Qays went on his own journey, one that he chose for himself. He knew he must struggle to earn Leyli. He refused food and stayed in the desert on the outskirts of town. The townspeople could hear his mad cries. He sang songs of strange beings in love who were dying on the beach with no water. His words were odd, his sounds off-key. They said he ate the dirt and the rocks and heat. They said he spoke to the snakes. Qays became "Majnun," meaning "crazy for love," to all but Leyli.

Leyli wandered, too, but within the city walls. She stayed away from her family. Even when at home, she remained outside, secluded in the walled-in family garden. She spent her months alone growing the garden into astounding lushness. Her mother said to her father in privacy, "It is like she has found a child now that her lover has gone."

After months, Majnun returned to the city. In its alleys, policemen beat him up, mistaking him for a thief.

When he arrived at Leyli's home, her father still refused to let Majnun see her. Too tired to fight, Majnun turned away. As he rounded the corner of the property, he heard a song, like a nightingale. He listened and knew that it sang his sound.

He climbed the high wall. On the other side was the garden. And Leyli.

Clinging to the top of the wall, Majnun called out to her. She didn't hear him. He fell, and the ground met him with a lover's embrace. Leyli kept on singing. She became famous but never married. She died a very old woman.

"Is that one better?" I ask her.

"Yes," she says. "It's more like how I told it." She stares at this ten-year-old playing Frisbee with his cocker spaniel. "But I told it better."

"What's wrong with it?"

"Oh, it's not your fault," my mother sighs. "You just don't have enough poetry in you. It's your American side. So, so—" Her voice trails off, and she gestures toward the boy and his dog. "In California, you won't let Faraz surf, will you? It's dangerous."

"Don't worry. He knows how to swim."

"Does he know how to stop an earthquake?"

"What is it about my father?"

"Was he really a father to you, Massoud?" She eats some *torshi*, and makes her sour-eating face. "My secret is for the end of the day, when you are done talking. My secret is not about childish things."

A boy prince, the Prince of the World Before the World. He traveled the Great Blackness looking for something to fill the planet. He brought back a little bit of everything. Sparkling rings, nebulous clouds, novas, supernovas, black holes, wormholes. Dust and darkness. Everything in between. Except a sun, for he couldn't hold onto any of the younger stars, which were slippery things. So, he returned home with all the splendor of the universe and no light to see it by, no warmth by which to feel its beauty. He swore to his people that he would return with the fire. That's why the Prince of the World Before the World left again.

The Prince of the World Before the World discovered a planet made of water. When he came down onto it, he found women waiting for him. They told him they were sad and the water of the planet consisted solely of their tears. But the water was fresh, their tears without salt. The Prince didn't understand how that could be: sorrow was always accompanied by something else. *No*, the women said, *that is happiness. Sadness is pure.* He asked the pure ones where he could find a fire that he could take home with him. The women just cried.

The Prince of the World Before the World discovered a planet made of earth. The Prince found it strange, the dirt. On his planet, the ground was made of sand. Earth resembled sand but was darker and moister. The Prince relished its difference. He felt that fire must be nearby because this earth looked burned. He called out. The earth itself vibrated in answer. The Prince wrote out a message in the dirt. The earth erased it, and responded in like manner: *Fire is inside me.* When the Prince asked if he might have some, the land began to break apart.

Whether the earth was angry or accommodating, the Prince could not tell. He had to leave or die.

The Prince of the World Before the World discovered a planet made of wind that moved nothing. He found all the trees young because they did not need to grow, to age. The Prince listened and he could hear the wind. He could hear it well. He thought he felt it, too. He asked the leaves if they could feel the wind. *Of course, silly*, they said. He asked the leaves why then they did not move. *We don't know this word, move.* The Prince jumped up and down. *Only the wind moves. If we move, we become the wind.* Perplexed, the Prince asked the leaves where he could find a fire he could take home with him. The leaves asked their young trees, who screamed in horror. They told the Prince that Mother Wind had banished fire long ago to a place far away in the Great Blackness. The Prince asked where, and the young trees told him they did not want to know.

The Prince of the World Before the World hovered in the Great Blackness, facing everywhere the stars he could not conquer. He discovered there was no planet made of fire. This is why the Prince of the World Before the World never returned. But he was warm out there. And safe. Like the young trees, he had no need to age.

My mother wrinkles her nose. "When did I tell you that one?"

"In second grade," I tell her. "I was home with the chicken pox, and you were feeding me four oranges a day."

"Oranges are good for you when you're sick."

"Do you remember the story?" I ask.

"No, but does it matter?" she asks. "If you remember it, then it's important, like a dream. Maybe Baha'u'llah wants you to remember for a reason."

I recite:

"O SON OF MAN!

"Write all that We have revealed unto thee with the ink of light upon the tablet of thy spirit. Should this not be in thy power, then make thine ink of the essence of thy heart. If this thou canst not do, then write with that crimson ink that hath been shed in My path. Sweeter indeed is this to Me than all else, that its light may endure for ever."

"I'm glad you remember God," my mother says.

And then I am my mother, speaking: "I met your father when I was at Baha'i school in North Carolina. I heard his voice even before I saw him. I knew, I knew I was going to marry him. His voice was so calm. I asked Amanda to introduce us. He said he fell in love with my hair.

"Then, I had to go back to Augusta. He was on a military base in Colorado because he was drafted. He wrote me letters. These letters were so beautiful. You can't believe it, Massoud. I'll show you if you want me to. He wrote letters for years until the army let him go.

"The letter when he proposed I read to everybody in the E.R., and they all said, 'No wonder you cry when you read these letters.' Even the doctors said so.

"Still, your father wanted to ask my father for permission. So, he sent his letter to Iran. He wrote one to his parents. I also sent a letter to my parents and his parents. Everyone asked permission. We were worried the letters from Iran wouldn't come back in time for May, but they did.

"It was the worst day. The cake melted. I should have known then."

Having finished the story, I ask my mother. "Do you remember your own words?"

"Those are *your* words," she says. "It's true the wedding wasn't so good, but I always told you I didn't care. I loved your father."

"Is that your secret? Or is the *opposite* your secret? You cannot keep this from me."

"My secret has nothing to do with hurt. I loved your father."

But her words killed him a long time ago, not with anger. With something else.

ഋൟ

A woman in a hooded white robe enters. Everyone stares at her. She is the first goddess. Light and pain emit from her core, and seconds later everyone is dead. She is the last goddess. And the best.

When I was eleven, I dreamt that my mother died at the hospital where she worked. In my dream, I saw her walking down a hospital corridor, toward the white light of death, indiscernible from that of the hospital. My mother was wearing her white uniform, too. After this, I was certain my mother really was going to die at work. I was young enough to believe.

I'm not sure why I was so afraid of my mother dying, but often, I pretended to be sick so she would stay home.

When I got older, I pretended to be well.

Now, she is retired. I should be relieved because I still believe in that dream. I am not relieved. Now, I am afraid my mother will never die.

A barren landscape. People made of stone. What could wake them? They are still and cold if you dare to touch them. One day, a traveling salesman came through with a lamp. Whatever stone its light touched melted into flesh. The traveling salesman was so frightened he left without the lamp. The Stone People, now melted, wandered aimlessly for a while, but after a few days, one of their young took charge. He realized the value of the lamp. After a few weeks, however, so did everyone else. Every merchant who came through wished to "pay respects" by adorning the lamp with jewels or gold.

One day a messenger came from the King. He told the Stone People that the King was confiscating the lamp because it was so precious. The Stone People possessed no weapons, so they couldn't prevent the King's men from taking the lamp.

At the palace, the King adorned the lamp with more and

more jewels. He placed it in the court, inside a glass case. Followers came from far and wide to see the Wonderlamp.

The Stone People quickly turned back into rocks, boulders.

Eventually, the King tired of the Wonderlamp. It fell into the hands of merchants, then thieves who stripped it bare of wealth.

Then, one day. . .

A traveling salesman arrived with a lamp. People made of stone were warmed by its light. As stone, their dreams were light. Had they finally become their dreams? Perhaps, but we must wait for the King to come again.

"I remember this one," my mother says. "I didn't write it. It's a book you had. I think it was called *The Wonderlamp*."

"You told me I didn't have books when I was younger."

"Well, one or two," she says. "This one was good and clean. The stone people are the faithless."

"So, God is a lamp?" I ask.

"No, no. It's a story."

"Can light make stone into flesh, the dead into the living?"

My mother sighs, and says, "If it's supposed to be the light of God."

"And does the light of God make life?"

"Yes."

"And does it make love?"

"Yes." She stands up with a little effort and shields her eyes so she can look across the sunny field. After a moment, she turns to me to tell me about a news story that she saw about an earthquake, about the poor and the poorly constructed homes. About how no one knows what to do. She asks me if I know what to do. I tell her that I know to stand in the doorway. Then, I just stare, still stuck on the field and this day. I wonder why no one is flying kites. The wind is so elegant today.

Mullah Nasr al-din was a rich man who would go to the public square and give away his money. Yet, he often borrowed items from those who lived near him. One day, he borrowed a pot from one of his neighbors.

In this pot, Nasr al-din cooked *fesenjaan*, which was very good. Then, he returned the pot.

Inside, the owner found a smaller pot. The neighbor said, "Nasr al-din, you only borrowed one pot."

Nasr al-din replied, "Yes, but the pot was pregnant."

Again, Nasr al-din borrowed a bigger pot, but from a different neighbor. He cooked *ghormeh sabzi*, which was very good. Then, he returned the pot.

Inside the owner found another pot, though this pot inside the pot was larger than the first one. Again, the initial pot was pregnant.

And so, Nasr al-din kept borrowing bigger and bigger pots.

Until one day, he borrowed the biggest pot in town. He cooked many things, which were all very good. Then, he returned the pot. But without another pot inside it. This neighbor said, "Nasr al-din, was this pot not pregnant, too?"

Nasr al-din replied, "Yes, but the child died at birth."

My mother recites the punch line with me. "That one I love. It used to be my father's favorite."

I don't have a picture of my grandfather. I never met him. He died when I was six. My father answered the phone and silently handed the phone to my mother. I like to think in that silence I knew something was wrong. But it was my father who had the courage to hold my mother as she cried and shook. Part of her grief was knowing she couldn't go to the funeral, couldn't go back to Iran because she was Baha'i.

She told me once years later that the grave, like many Baha'i graves, had been lost, built upon. So, if we ever want to visit his grave, we'll have to enter an office building, a gas station, or maybe someone else's home. This is what it means to have family. The dead require you to enter someone else's home. My family is my own. The dead are dead.

༄༅

Uncle Mahmed falls in love with an American girl. They have a beautiful baby girl and name her Jessica.

After many years of working hard, Mahmed slows down. He begins to look around. Jessica has grown. Silky black hair, eyes like his own mother's. But his wife, the American girl, won't allow Mahmed to sit still. Money, she demands. He obeys because he doesn't know what else to do. The American girl demands so rarely. So, Mahmed believes her actions sincere and justified. He works hard.

Years later, he has no friends. He works for IBM, and at home all he does is surf the Internet for odd pieces of knowledge. The American girl eats ice cream and doesn't move when he touches her. Through Jessica, his mother's eyes chide him: *I told you to marry a nice Persian girl.*

"Did you get the bonus?" the American girl asks.
"Yes."
"Did you get the bonus?" the American girl asks.
"Yes."
"Did you get the bonus?" the American girl asks.
"Yes."

When they have been married for six years, Mahmed notices the American girl spending many nights out with her friends. He knows her secret. Still, upon confronting her and hearing her confession, Mahmed senses the piercing pain of his mother's god.

That weekend, while his wife shops and his daughter is at a friend's house, he hangs himself.

"It was such a tragedy," my mother says.

"You know," I say, "in *The Divine Comedy*, the spirits of suicides are captured in young trees."

"I don't know anything about this comedy," my mother says. "I don't think it sounds very funny."

"He was only your second cousin, right?"

"It's a lesson," she says. "His sisters and his mother told him not to marry her. They loved him and knew best. You should have listened to me before you got married."

"But you married an American, too," I say.

"It's not about American," she yells. "It's about believing in God, being good and clean. That wife of yours, I need to teach her. She would probably go outside for ice cream during an earthquake."

I tell my mother that my wife isn't a child, and my mother says that we're all children until someone we love dies.

There was a young girl who walked on walls. She proved thus her courage. Always, however, the young girl wanted to jump off the wall. Most girls her age wanted to fly up into the sky, but she wanted to fly down at the ground. The earth itself was foreign to her the way the sky was to many of her friends.

Day after day, the girl climbed up the wall and walked its perimeter. She stopped at various points to study the ground.

Earth whispered to her: *Jump.*

The father saw his daughter as some sort of bird, perched on their garden wall constantly. He knew you could not force a bird to come to you. Rather, you had to entice the bird with a treat. Over the next days and weeks, he scattered various seeds on the ground.

The young girl remained on the wall.

Earth sang her songs, melodious and in need of no words. She swayed in rhythm atop the wall.

The father became frightened for his daughter's life. As he paced their home, his wife asked him what troubled him. He told her of the problem and his failed solution. She laughed at him. Little girls are not birds. The mother scattered apricot slices on the ground because she knew little girls liked apricots.

The young girl remained on the wall.

Earth increased the volume and speed. The young girl danced maniacally.

The parents consulted a wise man. He told them to leave their daughter alone. So, they did.

The little girl remained on the wall.

Earth got tired and silent.

One day, soldiers came and took the parents away. They did not see the little girl atop the wall.

The little girl remained on the wall.

Months and months. Strange plants began to grow. The garden lost its shape. The little girl could no longer see the ground. *Oh, Father, what have you done?* She jumped to the earth, fearing she could not make it through the plant growth. And yet her body hit with such force that Earth shook, bled even as she bled. Like seeds and apricots, the young girl became part of the mayhem.

My mother has stormed off and now stands in the field underneath the sun at some distance from me. Could she have heard my story, my whispering? I know she loved him. It's myself I'm unsure of, my love for my parents I'm unsure of.

A postcard. Painting of an old conquest, which hangs in a building named for its pillars. Twenty pillars . . . forty, sixty, eighty, one hundred. No, just twenty but known for twice that. In a building made of mirrors, multiplication is necessary.

Math. Ayyám-i-Há. Days outside of time. On the postcard, Mother writes to Father about Baha'i holidays, about missing him, about love—in her broken English. Her English, like her stories, piecemeal. She buries my head in the sand with her stories. Down there, it's silver and gold, pure blue, shattered glass.

Here and now, in a place much too close, a place surrounded by hills, a son and a mother picnic. She is old and tired but still filled with hopes. He struggles to understand too many things.

When the son was a child, his mother told him stories, as most mothers do. Except most of her stories didn't originate in books. So, the son eventually came to believe his function was to remember these stories. He always thought he would need to pass them on. Instead, today he tries to return these stories.

The son himself became a father. And then the son's own father passed away. The son began to wonder what the father's duty was. The son was plagued with guilt at the frivolity of his mother's stories and at his trouble remembering them. Making a story matter is impossible, though, and trying to remember is like waiting for birds to eat from your palm.

His own father never told him a single story.

The son realized too slowly how much he loved his own father. The son realized too slowly as he viewed his father's varnished body that the recognizable always eludes you. But the struggle satisfies. He realized too slowly as he viewed his father's varnished body that his relationship with his father was, is, as intimate as it gets. Neither God nor a lover can compare. He realized too slowly as he viewed his father's varnished body that the father's best duty is that of real absence. The mother is always telling stories. The father is always unknown. In death now, the father shows the son what a story is, desire. To know, not remember. Without the father here, his life opens to interpretation, and the father's own stories scribble themselves out so slowly. And these tales are true and relevant, present and in the present.

Even as the son struggles to know his father, his mother's stories interfere. He wonders how to keep his own son safe. He will tell his own son that stories never aid in reality, that the best stories *are* real.

Today, the son will return his mother's stories, and he'll be successful. Years from now, his own son will look at him and say, "Father, tell me the story of your life." And the once son and now father will begin in language made of wood and earth, a language that his son cannot refuse.

"Those aren't my stories," my mother says, returning to her seat on the blanket. She begins packing up the food.

"Then, where did they come from?" I ask.

She eats the last *dolmeh* and turns around to gauge the distance back to the car.

"You don't understand," I say. "All stories are unhealthy."

"You're doing good, and you heard plenty of stories."

"I'm not doing well."

"What's wrong?" My mother crumples a napkin, waiting. "You're too serious," she says, "like your father."

"There's nothing wrong with that."

"Stories," she says, "they make it right."

"Make what right?" I ask.

"Stories are for loneliness," she says. "Like when you are going to leave me all alone. Like when your father did."

"He died of a heart attack. He didn't leave." She confuses me once again. "You told me about that day, that day when he died."

"But what is a heart attack?" she asks. She stares up at the sun and then rubs her eyes. "No nurse can tell you what you want to know. I'll mail you his death certificate after you leave for California. Then, you will have to come back and tell me the true story."

My grandfather was fifty-two years old when he died. He died in the bathtub, slipped and hit his head. I think of how the last thing he saw was white plastic. Or maybe the bathtubs in Iran are stone, marble. Still, it was a good, clean way to die.

But this isn't the truth. He died in a hospital.

What lie has she told me? What lie is she telling me? These things happen when you try to tell a story. Important details slip away, and eventually, you're left not knowing what killed your father. What will someday come for your mother, who has made herself the goddess of stories, the goddess of an irresistible story. She always wins.

My mother shakes her black hair, gray at the roots, and says with a mouth full of food, "Your problem is that you never listen."

I try to listen to this world. I really do. But before my very eyes, my mother's hair becomes the wind and carries her away. A stream of blood trails behind, whispering to me of old lives and new deaths—of *her* story. The lustful imagination of a raw grape leaf in one's mouth. The hateful reality of a sunny day. And I know it is left to me to tell the stories, all of them.

Listen to This

Mom sent me to the store to get change for tomorrow because the change machine at the Laundromat hasn't worked since I was ten. And the path takes me right by the Paynes' place on Palmetto. I try to feel something about their murders—the invasion of privacy and the destruction of our sense of security—but all I can do is wish it were next year and I had my driver's license so that the next time Mom asked me to go to the store in this heat, it wouldn't take so long. The only other people walking around are drug addicts who woke up confused and decided to walk it off. I guess anything is better than sitting still. At least Mom doesn't make me go with her to the Laundromat anymore. A fifteen-year-old boy doesn't belong in a Laundromat. The Paynes could do their laundry at home.

In the 7-11, I have to wait while the cashier, Kingston, tries to educate a customer about how it's the mass media that's created sociopaths and serial killers. The customer says he doesn't watch the news because it's depressing. Kingston says apathy is the worst kind of wildfire, but it never gets featured on network news. The customer squints and asks Kingston if he knew the Paynes. He didn't, and the customer says it's a shame. They were good people. There goes the neighborhood.

Now this, this makes sense to me: There goes the neighborhood. My dad talks like Kingston, uses words like *bemoan*. Dad said just last week that it was easy to bemoan the invasion of privacy if you believed in privacy, and only homeowners could believe in privacy. And privacy was just a different way of locking your door. Mom nodded and said, "Exactly," but I didn't get it, and this slow-rising anger struck me, as usual. There goes the neighborhood, though, that's enlightening. The Paynes are just gone. There they go. See you later. And there's something beautiful in that.

I hand Kingston the ten dollar bill. He opens the register and starts counting out the quarters. "Haven't seen your dad lately. He quit drinking?"

"No, he's out of town, visiting his sister because she's sick." This is what my mother has told me to say. And you can't tell a lie if you don't know the truth.

Kingston nods, but I know he doesn't care. He could never keep up with my dad, even when Dad was drunk. "You seen what they did to the Payne place?" He doesn't wait for my answer. "They got police tape all around it, marking the perimeter of the property, like it's some exhibit in a museum."

I don't tell him half of the tape's been ripped down because that would get him started on some rant about desecration. Probably holiness, too. "Yeah, I saw it," I say. "It's real sad."

"No," Kingston says, "a travesty." He scoops the quarters into a small brown bag for me.

On the walk home, I hold the bag close and tight so the quarters won't jingle.

At home, my mother is waiting on water to boil for green beans. She sits there, smoking a Virginia Slims 120 and reading some intellectual book, something about crying. There are too many intellectuals in this town.

"Josh, listen to this," my mom says. Then, she reads me something about time and timelines and lining up lives.

Something about a chorus and harmony. I'm grateful, as always, that my older sister, Lily, reads *Cosmo*. Plus, she really knows about music.

My mom is grinning at me, waiting for me to say something elusive, like "Harmony is only as beautiful as its dissonance." I just ask her where Lily is. Mom points to the screen door. Out there on the back balcony, Lily practices for her drum major tryouts. I stand here, watching. Mom comes up behind me and starts crying. Lily always makes Mom cry. Lily's mere presence. Mom says it's because she's proud of Lily, her first-born and a fellow female, but I think it's more than that. Fear, perhaps. Or recently, also shame. Mom leans against the counter and sobs quietly as she drops the beans into the water.

But Lily, she's fine out there. Masterful, if you ask me. Being a drum major, conducting, is more than just keeping the rhythm. It's crescendos and decrescendos, cues, not flinching when the oboes squeak or the melaphones go flat. It's about making prairie grass glide-step into a nontraditional formation from the third-floor balcony of a low-income apartment building. Dad always said this place was a shithole. Only true thing he ever said. I hope he figured it all out. I hope he never comes back.

The daylight is almost gone, that last ray disappearing slow enough to be noticed. Lily keeps going. Her body is rigid except for her head and arms. She won't let the night alone. It can close her up, but she won't wonder at its darkness or, as Kingston would say, signify. Lily tries to fill the night with something tangible. Even now, I can almost hear some minor-key melody about loneliness. But there is nothing, nothing, nothing in the air except my sister's hands. Behind me, Mom is at the kitchen table again. "Josh," she says, wiping her tears, "listen to this."

Heart of a Locust

My son runs into the wind, and his shirt billows out behind him. He says he will sail away. I grab his arm, hard, and pull him away from the wind, from the street, from the cars in the street.

"That hurt," Jake says. "Too hard."

"I told you about running," I say. "You can't run. It's dangerous. Only on the playground."

"There aren't any cars. I looked."

"It's always the car you don't see."

He squirms and squiggles, using his body weight against me. He's too young to know how to use his body. Years from now, he will come home drunk, and I'll remember this seemingly drunken walk down 4th, past the bakery, the independent bookstore, the paint-your-own-pottery shop. All the way to the clinic on the corner, where they'll swab our cheeks and compare us on trays where our parts will become, as they describe it, glow-y—I think separate and luminous, luminous like those deep-sea creatures that I saw on television one night, late when the house was quiet. Then, they'll help me figure out who Jake's father is. I was too young then, and I'm too young now. When I was a teenager, my grandmother said that Man's heart was evil from his youth. When

I was a teenager, I told her that I was no evil thing. She said that
God always got the first and last Word. My grandmother's got an
unwavering faith, but her way of speaking and worshipping has
changed. Now, she's more inspirational than damning. Now, I'm
twenty-something and potentially evil-hearted. My grandmother
thinks Jake's father was my first, that I should know who the
father is. I couldn't tell her.

She's at home getting ready for the "senior" prom at church
tonight. She has a handsome date, a Sean Connery look-alike.
My grandmother is starting all over. She says we all need to
start over, start living for real and not like a bunch of old
rock'n'roll stars trying to make it big with a twilight-year
comeback. Grandmother says we need to purge and then go
after what we want, what we need. She's going after true love,
the second time around. She's told me that I must go to a
community college in the area. Grandma always said that I was
smart before—before the you-know, which is my own mother's
crazy. I don't remember being smart, but Grandma says that I
was creative-smart. She says I was smart and against-smart at
the same time. I asked her if against-smart isn't the same as
dumb, and she said, "It's smart like a dream." Grandma says
that we can do it. I believe her because she dyed her hair and
bought a sexual lubricant. She says that I have to hold down a
job first. I just got fired from the Golden Corral. But I also
believe that to purge your past you must know it. I know that
my mother is dying, up at the loony bin—because she tried to
kill herself one too many times, without succeeding, except this
time she succeeded, sort of, but it will be a slow death—and I
don't know who Jake's father is. I need to know, and then it's
living for real.

Jake wakes me up in the middle of the night. He says goblins
exist, no matter how much I say they don't. He says he had this
dream again, that they came to him. Just now. The goblins came
to him and said if his father ever came home, they would take

him, Jake, away from me. I tell Jake his father isn't so bad. Jake
says he wishes he could believe me. He says that I won't even
let him listen to the radio. Is his father famous? No, I tell him.
The radio is just a bad influence. I tell Jake that he's too young
to worry about this, restrictions and all. I'll worry about his
father, how to get him home.

Jake says a purple goblin told him to sneak into my bedroom
and put a pillow over my face. I ask Jake if he thinks that's
funny. He says that this is really what he dreamt. He knows it's
wrong. He loves me. I tell him to go back to sleep. Jake asks if
we can talk more about goblins tomorrow. I leave him to sleep,
and I go outside to stare at the broken wooden fence, the dry
grass, and the kiddie pool. And the moon. The dry and broken
wooden moon. And I think of my mother, how it will feel when
she dies. Much like it already does?

A nightmare of my own: A goblin kills my mother, but the
goblin is me. She lies on an operating table, wrapped with white
cloth, like a mummy, roses in between her skin and the cloth
because I can smell them.

Then, she is there, skiing on the broad, white mountains
with a shock of color behind her. I thought I had killed her, but
now she chases me. What is that color? What rainbow? What
say you, goblin?

My mother is yelling something. She is yelling for her own
mother to save her as she races down the slope, toward what—
a wall or a tree or a burst of light.

"How was prom?" I ask Grandma the next morning.

"Oh, you know," she says. "All that peach schnapps. The
sugar's what does you in."

Her auburn hair doesn't glow in the morning sun, and she
doesn't look flushed or happy, even hungover. She looks like an
old lady.

"Something happen with Sean Connery?"

"Ted, and no. We had a nice evening." She has her back to me, and the water pours into the yellow kettle with a sound that's like an echo off a distant cliff face.

"Did he make a pass at you?" I say, smiling like a fiend.

She turns. Her face is smaller, then, and I think she's about to cry. But this could all be a trick of morning light. "It was a nice evening," she says.

Can a face fold into itself? That's what it looks like. I touch her arm, to comfort. The water is still running behind us, the kettle overflowing.

She says I need to go see my mother before she dies. Grandma's been three times. I don't want to go to the hospital. My mother's in a coma anyway, and there's this psychiatrist from the loony bin hanging around because he's using Mom in his study on the genetics of suicide. I tell Grandma that there's no point. I speak too loudly, and even though she's the one crying, she looks at me with pity.

"I should lust not. On my grave, they'll write *Kibroth hattaavah*," she says.

Grandma has been alone for a long time. In her youth, she had her husband, a naval corpsman. Then, she had Mother, and, now, me and Jake. Alone, though surrounded by us. Alone *because* surrounded by us.

I have been alone for a long time—really alone. I worry about my son, his dreams and his hair that's too long and the father he's never had but just might need. And of course, I don't want to be alone—or leave anyone alone.

I've worked at the Winn Dixie, the Radio Shack, the Golden Corral, the Belk's, and the Tom Thumb gas station. I've been fired for chewing gum, cursing, flashing customers, mooning bosses, not refilling the sweet tea on time, and not using the counterfeit detection pen on large bills. I just got a job at the Pleaze-U gas station and convenience store. To get the job, I flashed the manager, Mr. Josh, as we're to call him.

ৎৡৡ

A picture of Grandma. She lounges on a beach chair. Her hair is done up for a special occasion, but she's at the beach. All around her, sand. The sand is white in the black and white photo. She is lounging on a dark chair in a sea of light. Her hair, dark. Her shadow is the third object. Grandma doesn't look into the camera. She looks away and up. She looks directly at the sun, for you can see its light in her eyes. Her eyes are white. She is beautiful. She has pale skin, but smooth. She has her bikini on, the kind with shorts for a bottom, but her stomach is exposed and flat. Her breasts are full. She has applied her lipstick just so, a darker shade. Maybe red. The only other makeup I notice is a beauty mark that I know isn't natural. I scratch at the photo, trying to take it away.

Sometimes when I look at these old pictures, I wonder about how beauty fades. Grandma says that you can always see beauty, if it was ever there. But I look at her, and I know that it can fade, that it can be something left behind in pictures, not of our flesh.

At the Pleaze-U, you—oh yes, *you*—have to pre-pay after nine o'clock. Customers stand outside taking their time figuring this out, even though there's a sign with bold font on each pump. My co-worker, Mary Beth, who is only seventeen, asks me if I've got a man. I tell her that I've got a little man, named Jake. We get to talking about how men are shit, and Mary Beth lifts up her Pleaze-U smock and her shirt underneath and shows me where some guy came on her stomach, and because she didn't wash the next day and there was something wrong with his cum, now she has little red rashes all over her belly. Mr. Josh comes strolling by, and Mary Beth quickly re-clothes herself. Then, her face crumples like Grandma's and she cries a little bit. I start to tell her the story of my dream. I ask her what it all means. Mary Beth says to ask someone older. I tell her I want to know what she thinks. After I ring up a thirty-ounce slushy for some kid with blue hair, Mary

Beth says that my mother was running toward *me*, that I am the burst of light. I tell her that I was the goblin, and Mary Beth says that I don't get dreams at all.

The genetics of suicide: Seretonergic pathway. Intronic polymorphisms. MAOA. Life. Love. Money. Family. One man and one woman, and then children.

The genetics of suicide, if laid out on a plate, are like a fancy meal at the steak house. You cannot say what you like best, but it all just works together on your palate. A delight which leads you to heights of ecstasy, and despair that you will never eat that meal again. That singular moment, when your son walks a certain way, your mother smiles a certain way, when a boy touches you a certain way. Now, it's not about the certainty, but the uncertainty that you will ever experience *this* again, the joy in that. Monsters and mutations. Separate but luminous.

I've got the afternoon off, and Jake and I are going back to the clinic today for a consultation that I requested. Jake isn't very clear on what's going on, and I intend to keep it that way. Grandma is at a makeup party.

Inside, there are mostly couples, men and women who look tired and who do not look at each other. Jake isn't the only child there. In the corner, three other kids play with a pretend oven. They keep confusing who is the cook, the server, the customer. I see one woman who was here last time. She wears her lipstick old-fashioned, so there are two pointy peaks on top. She's alone. I can't remember if she was with someone last time.

Jake scoffs at the younger kids playing restaurant. I sign us in, and the woman behind the counter leans over to look at Jake. "How old are you?" she asks. I tell her he's seven. "We have some educational magazines, and they're real fun."

I drag him away before he can be rude.

"When we leave, can we go get fries?" Jake asks.

"Fries and hamburgers?"

He says, "I don't feel like eating meat. Grandma says that the meat is full of hormones. She says I could go crazy."

"Meat is fine, Jake. Don't listen to everything your grandma says."

"She's really my great-grandma, right?" he asks. I say yes, and he says, "If she were my grandma *and* your grandma—that would mean we have the same mother."

"Jake, stop messing around."

"I'm just saying. If you weren't my mother, I think my mother would have blonde hair, blonde hair like a movie star. Then, I'd have blonde hair, too, and we would live in a house with a real pool."

This is one difficulty of parenthood: to punish by wrath or silence. Another is to know how to love your child.

The kid across from us swings his legs. I think of the swing sets of my childhood, the one in the park, the one Mom took me to before she went to Betton. And I think of swinging hard and launching up through the clouds to that place Grandma always said was not quite heaven but dreamy enough.

When Jake was four, he began to dream of monsters. These monsters were purple and they ate people. I told him that was a song. He said, "What song?" His favorite color was purple.

When I was pregnant with him, I lived with my grandmother, and she played all those old records. Grandpa's collection, really, but she couldn't get rid of it. When he died in Betton, years before I was born, she gave away everything except his records. She kept his records.

Jake looks like my grandfather. Grandma wishes that Grandpa and my mother could have known Jake. But they were gone, one really and one gone enough.

My mother used to make the best potato salad.

When Jake was four, he also began to dream of goblins. Some of them were purple and some red, yellow, green. I told him this was his favorite book, *Rainbow Goblins*. Jake said, "No, these are my dreams. And the goblins are coming."

❧

After Vietnam, Grandpa came home and tried to relax. He had lost too much, and he never really could love my mother.

He couldn't help but feel he'd traded the lives of his platoon's dead for his beautiful girl. He found some evil in her, and he felt he'd sold his soul, made that trade with the devil. When he'd left for the war, she was the pure and innocent babe. Now, she was Woman, at age four. Woman, this kind of beauty, was evil. He'd traded the lives of good and honest men for this sort of beauty. This sort of beauty led men to death, brought death to them. He'd made a trade.

The leafy green, the wet leaves, breathing. The sound of animals he couldn't name, bird sounds and larger and louder.

He had killed, but he had wanted to save.

He couldn't eat pot roast or pork butt or meatloaf or tuna casserole or even grilled cheese sandwiches. He wanted the meat of a locust. He wanted the heart of a locust, to be hard and hungry and to be able to live with what he had done.

He lit fires in the backyard and then he lit fire to cats that hung around. He cried. He said he would keep on until he stopped crying. Grandma said that a burning cat sounds unholy, like a siren that would never go off.

Then, Grandpa went bat-shit crazy. I wasn't born yet. Grandma was young enough to still be beautiful, and my mother was eight years old.

Grandma told me this when I was eighteen. She cried and told me that I should know the way of things.

The clinic counselor says, "I'm glad you set up this appointment." She flips through my file, stops and looks right at Jake. "Jake, I think you should have your own meeting with my friend who really wants to meet you."

"He can stay," I say.

"Come with me," the counselor says.

"He can stay," I say, and grab Jake's arm.

"Too hard, Mom," Jake whines.

I let go quickly, ashamed. And Jake is led out of the room, through the sterile hallways.

The counselor returns, and I feel strange without Jake. My chest opens up, and my breath comes easier. But I'm afraid while my body isn't. I hate this woman for taking him away.

"Sorry, but I don't discuss these things with children in the room," she says. "Well, Ms. Ellison, we have your sample and your child's. You've paid your down payment and partial collection fee for your son. But we can't really do anything until we have the potential father's DNA to compare to." She flips through the file. "Am I right in understanding that you don't have any candidates for the paternity test?"

"I don't know who the father is," I say. "Possibilities, but I don't know where those guys are. I don't have money for a P.I."

"Have you tried basic Internet searches and networking amongst your friends and acquaintances?"

"Yes."

"Well, we have a service that we recommend to our customers for a minimal fee. Basically, someone—not necessarily a P.I., now—does some legwork for you. The fee is much less than that of a P.I." She leans in. "And our guy is slick. It's a steal."

I wish I were at the makeup party with Grandma.

I agree, and the counselor takes down my information, and her slick not-a-P.I. is off to find Dylan Rosko.

A picture of Jake. He rides on his unicycle, which he insisted on for his fifth birthday. He mastered it, didn't fall off much at all. I told him he could have a regular bike, but he didn't want one. This kid was crazy for the unicycle. He said it was the only thing that could outrun the goblins.

The goblins were after him for what he knew not. Jake said, "They're like dogs after the mailman." Jake said the goblins were like a rainbow that he'd seen in science class, like all sorts of flowers, like pretty monsters. He said he wanted to play with them. I said, "Sure, play with your pretty monsters."

ஒஇ

Grandma walks through the door, and I can smell her makeup before I see it. I love the way her makeup has a smell. All the makeup I buy is hypoallergenic and good for my skin. But it's boring. Grandma has color and smell. Once a long time ago, I tasted her lipstick and it was candy.

"How was it?" I yell, before I can even see her.

"Wonderful. Just what I needed." She walks into the room, and her hair shines. "I love this eyeshadow."

"Lovely."

"I do feel a bit silly for my worldly desires, but it feels good, and it feels good to feel silly for once." She starts showing me what she bought for me. I refuse to go to these parties, mainly because of Rachel who is really and truly a whore and yet called me one when she didn't know I was there just around the corner during Thanksgiving right before Jake was born. Grandma always buys me stuff. Sometimes, I actually use it.

"Have you thought more about going to see your mother?" she asks.

I flip open eyeshadows and powders and blushes—all the compacts I can find. I smell them. I stick my nose in eyeshadow, powder, blush, and inhale slowly, then exhale. Like I'm trying to prevent a panic attack, which I've never had but imagined. The panic stays inside my head, my eyes. I remember a day when my mother wore makeup, a day before, before.

Grandma is quiet for a moment. Then, she asks, "Do you want a sandwich? I can make you some grilled cheese."

I'm ready to say no, but Jake wanders in, says, "Can we have fries, too?"

We have grilled cheese and fries, the crinkly frozen kind that cook up nice.

I have to work the night shift again tonight. Me and Mary Beth are good at this shift. We don't mind the customers getting irritated about pre-paying, the silly drugged-up kids, or the prank calls.

Mary Beth asks after Jake. She asks after Grandma and my dreams. I tell her we're all okay. Then, I think to tell her about Jake's goblin dreams, and she says, "Oh, so it's a family affair?" I tell her the dreams, and she says that I should get Jake checked out by a psychiatrist. I tell her that it's all normal, but she says, "I mean, who even thinks about goblins any more? That's so old and not like old school. Old like maybe fairy tales?"

Mr. Josh comes by the store, even though he's not the manager on shift. He pours us coffee and says it's free. After he's gone, I watch Mary Beth act like the coffee is poison. I ask her if she's okay.

Dylan Rosko was the first boy I ever slept with, but I kept going back to him. In the beginning, he lusted after me because I hit him every time he said "bitch" to or about any girl. I punched him good and hard in the shoulder, sometimes the leg. I was a thirteen-year-old feminist.

He walked home with me the Thursday before school let out for the summer. He grabbed at an azalea bush and gave me purple-pink flowers. He said, "I'd buy you some, but that might be *patronizing*, right?" He braced himself for a punch. I grabbed his hand instead. Held it too tight. I always hold too tight.

At home, my mother was gone. She was just gone. Dylan and I went out to the garage and played pool. He lost, and I was so happy to beat a guy and a guy two years older. I was jumping up and down like a kid, and Dylan came at me. He kissed me and I'd never been kissed like that before. A boy had never touched my arms or my stomach, especially not my legs. He touched my shoulder blades, and I couldn't remember if anyone had ever touched my shoulder blades, even my mother. Somehow, he was touching me all at once, and he had this way of brushing the skin, touching those little hairs on my skin that were standing straight up for him. He didn't let his fingers sink in. I felt like he was a ghost, ghost-touching me. And it was easy enough to believe it was all safe and innocent. It was easy enough to relax and just enjoy it.

Then, he stopped kissing me and looked into my eyes. I thought he was going to tell me that I was pretty, the prettiest girl he'd ever seen. He said, "Do you want to do this?" I felt then that *this* would be better than being prettiest. It would have reality, proof of it. I wouldn't just disappear, ever.

"What do I do?" I asked.

"Just be calm," he said, "and hit me if anything hurts."

A picture of Dylan. He leans against his Toyota Tercel, making up for the lame car with his coolness, his body and face relaxed and taunting the camera to do the same. *Relax.* Behind him and the car is a fence, and then the high school soccer field. He never played soccer.

He holds a pack of cigarettes in his hand, his arms crossed, like he refuses to give away a smoke. The white daylight shows how dark his hair his, so black it's almost blue or purple, like a cartoon. His skin white enough to melt away into the sky.

"Dear heart," Grandma says in the morning, "are you really not going to see your mother?"

Jake has fallen asleep, though he's too old for afternoon naps. I've just woken up from my morning sleep, sleep from seven to noon. We sit outside in beach chairs in the summer sun, which is mild today. Grandma has made us each a Tom Collins. She says it's like lemonade but better.

"I don't want to see her," I say. "She's been about as big a part of my life as that man who was my father."

She prattles on and on about how it's not my mother's fault, a disease, and how I should care. She says, "You will feel alone, even though you think you'll be glad to. I know how hard it's been, but if you don't say goodbye, you'll feel alone forever."

I know she's tired of being caretaker, to Grandpa, Mom, and now me. We thought Grandpa was sick from Vietnam. We never thought it was in our genes. His genes. My genes. Our genes. Separate and luminous amongst us.

"Grandma, I don't know who Jake's father is."

She looks at me and says with a great deep breath, "We're all fornicators. We're not all of God. He didn't send us, and the only way for us to move through the world is to fornicate. I've already forgiven you."

"I have a list." I take my list out of my pocket. There are four candidates, four possibilities, because by the time I got pregnant with Jake, my fornication was all I had. Mom was gone to Betton. She'd already tried to kill herself four times, once at home. The boy who was with me all those years ago, Dylan. He took one look at my mother, her milkshake mouth. He guided me into the living room and sat me down on the floral couch, soft to the touch. Velvet. You could run your fingernails against it, opposite the direction of the fibers. Like a cat, I clawed the couch while Dylan called the paramedics. It never occurred to me that she was still alive, that I could or should sit with her. Try to wake her up. I would now. I would tell her that it was a dream and a song and a book and that we loved her, even Grandpa.

After that, Grandma cried all the time because she'd been living in her own house away from us and dating this guy, a Gregory Peck look-alike. She'd thought everything was fine. She was starting over. Now, she had to take care of Mom. Grandma was reminded of Grandpa, who was still alive but locked away in Betton. I think maybe she thought it was her fault. She got over it pretty quick, took us in. Grandma tried her best. But it all went bad for me. So, I have a list.

I hand it to Grandma. It's on some pink stationery that she gave me for my birthday. Grandma cries but still reads the names, trying to figure out if she remembers these guys. She says again she's forgiven me.

Here's a picture of my mother. She's with a man a bit shorter than she is. They're dancing. He seems reluctant, avoids the camera's eye. My mother looks at us dead on. She smiles like Broadway.

She has on her black dress, off the shoulder. This guy wears a suit but no tie. The lawn behind them is green, summertime. And this is daytime. They're dancing like lovers in the daytime.

"Dylan Rosko?" Grandma asks. "The one in jail?"

"Not anymore," I say, "and it was juvie. That was a long time ago."

"Michael Smith, Roberto Espinoza, Nick Ziedel." She refolds the list. "I don't remember any of them. Not really." She's still crying a little.

"I was good at keeping my secrets," I say.

"All of these could be Jake's father?" she asks. "How could that be?"

"Dr. Chaudary said that the window could be pretty wide, depending. He helped me calculate it so I could be sure." I take the list from her. "And I'm changing as we speak. So are you. We're going to start living for real, right?"

She sits up in her beach chair. She looks out at the brown yard. Now, Grandma is really crying. She takes this, my mother dying, harder than I do. She says that I dissociated, which is a term she gets from the doctors up at Betton. They want me to come in more, for Mom and for psychological tests. The whole study on the genetics of suicide. I want to tell them that it's not passed on. It's something people have to deal with, and sometimes people imitate. It's the sincerest form of flattery.

I say, "Don't worry." I take her hands. They shake a little. I am shocked by the dryness, the bones I feel through thin skin. I could break her by accident. I expect her to complain about my grip, like Jake always does, but she just lays her head on my shoulder.

A secret, revealed: My grandmother has interviewed with this doctor doing his genetic research on suicide. She said he asked her about Grandpa, and she told him about the schizophrenia and how he took a Saturday drive into the side of a brick building. Grandma said the doctor told her that it wasn't anyone's fault, that we can't fight genes. Grandma said that she found some relief in this, solace.

I told her that she should be ashamed. I told her that we are all together here, though there is a wall, and we are all above something—animals and weather, I don't know. But we are all up high. Perhaps, we all sit or stand atop it, I told her, but we are all together here. There are not those below in the genetic muck who we excuse from watching. Watch the sunset. Watch the dead, the *death* of the sunset, the bright sky, the green trees, the success of all Mankind.

At work again tonight with Mary Beth. Mr. Josh is on duty, and his buddy cop friend swings by to check on the store every hour. Mr. Josh goes out to meet him, and they laugh. Mary Beth says that she's tired and goes off to the bathroom for long periods of time. Then, whenever we start talking about something, she wanders off to stare at the display of Tab and pork rinds.

Mr. Josh swings by the counter and tells me that he likes my shirt. I say that it would look better if I took my Pleaze-U smock off. He says to go ahead, so I do, and right then, his cop friend drives up outside and honks while yelling things you would maybe hear at a football game. I still have my t-shirt on, so I don't know what the fuss is about.

Then, Officer Duvall is inside coming toward the fun. On his way in, he spots Mary Beth, now perched on top of the four-foot display of Tab, pork rinds to her right. Officer Duvall asks me how my grandmother and Jake are and if I remember that football game where he—and I say I don't. I pull my smock back on and nudge Mary Beth off the display.

After Duvall and Mr. Josh leave, Mary Beth looks like she's going to cry but doesn't. We are silent until the morning sun.

A picture of my mother. She sits with Grandma on a green settee. Grandma is younger. Mom is younger. Their hair shines.

Grandma's hair is light brown, and I can see its summer highlights. She wears it in a bob. Mom's hair is darker, like mine. She wears it long but in a ponytail. Grandma smiles picture-perfect, like a doll, for the camera. Mom smiles but she slouches, and I can tell she hates this. Still, she smiles.

When I look closer, I wonder if Grandma is really happy. Yes, she's really happy. Mom is okay, too. She slouches because she's a kid, not because she hates this. She's looks calm, too. I don't remember my mother ever sitting still. But here she seems good at it. Her slouch is her giving in to Grandma, to happiness or, no, maybe just the calm of the moment. Or maybe she was outside in the sun and the water all day. She's exhausted from happiness.

The next morning, Jake wakes me up at eleven. "I had another dream," he says. "About the goblins."

"And what did they tell you to do this time?" I ask.

"They said to take away Grandma's lipstick."

"Why?"

"I don't know," he says. "It looks weird."

"What if Grandma likes it?"

"She doesn't. She licks at it." Jake messes with the chair's plastic, sticks his fingers through and pulls them out. "She smells weird, too."

"Grandma needs to try different things," I say. "She's trying to be happy."

He's quiet, and I can relax and drink my Tom Collins now. But no, Jake's not done.

"The goblins say this isn't right. They say we have to, to take her away. I know you don't think the goblins are real. Maybe they aren't. But I don't understand what they are. They're real in my dreams. I understand them there. I know where they came from," he says. "I know what they want."

"Grandma's lipstick?"

"What they *really* want is different." I push his hair out of his face, and I see by his eyes and the shape of his lips that he's serious.

༄༅

The search service the counselor recommended has found a phone number for Dylan Rosko. It's a local number. But they only give you a phone number and an e-mail address so I don't know where he lives.

When I was twelve, I came home to find my mother with a gun in her hand. She didn't answer me when I asked her what was going on. I thought she was mad at me. I thought she was trying to punish me. I'd just stolen eight dollars from her purse that morning. I thought she'd found out and was going to scare me straight. But no matter what I said, she didn't answer me. She didn't even look up from the yellow vinyl of the tabletop. I sat down next to her. I put my hand on hers. She didn't respond. I said, "Mom, what are you doing?" And she said, "I don't know. I remember us being a family. Your father loved you. He told me that I was crazy, and then I felt crazy." I felt her hair, to make sure she was real. I brushed it out of her face. I wondered if that's what it felt like to love someone. I thought I should hug her, but I didn't. I kept my hands on the tabletop. Yellow, like the sun that should always cheer us up. We sat there for about thirty minutes, me watching her for any sign of movement.

Eventually, I took the gun away from her, and she didn't respond. I took it into the other room with me. I called Grandma.

Grandma walked into the kitchen and saw Mom just sitting there. Grandma tried to get through to her, too, but nothing worked. Mom spent a few weeks at Betton, and when she came back, she hugged me and said that she was sorry that she'd "flipped out." Stress, my mother said. Then, we made brownies and she joked about how glad she was that I'd come home that day. "Imagine if I'd done it," she said. "What a mess!" Maybe I started to cry then. My mother hugged me and said she was sorry and she would never do that to me again. She told me to remember that people, like Dad, left her. She told me she'd never left anyone, not really. I knew she told the truth.

ৡৡ

We're making spaghetti and turkey meatballs for dinner. Grandma doesn't cook with beef anymore. Jake is making the meatballs too big, says he can eat them all. He needs big meatballs. The size of softballs.

"Listen," Grandma says, "if you're okay with raw meat in the middle, you can make them as big as you want."

Jake splits his big meatballs in half.

"I found out where Dylan is," I say to Grandma.

"I told you that it doesn't matter," she says.

"Who's Dylan?" Jake asks.

"It matters to me. I need to know"

"Why?" Grandma asks.

"I don't want to be alone with Jake."

"But Grandma's here," Jake says.

"It's a different sort of lonely," I say. "Don't you feel it, too?"

Grandma hushes us before we can begin to speak, for real, about Jake's missing father. Grandma redirects us, our attention, back to food and board games. Jake wants to know what hormones are, and if they're in his meat, what will they do to him? Grandma speaks, then, of illness and insanity.

A picture of my father. He's sitting on a bench, and his hair has gone gray. He has elbows on the table, hands folded together. He's about to tell us something. I can't see his eyes clearly because his glasses are bright with the flash and other reflected light. The trees are blurred in the wind behind him. The bench is painted red, and I can see people have already carved themselves into it. Maybe *Johnnie loves Katie.* I've never been here, and I don't remember him looking like this. But he's about to tell us something.

I'm working the eight-to-midnight shift at the Pleaze-U. At Grandma's insistence, I brought some meatballs for Mary Beth. Grandma says Mary Beth sounds like she could use a good meal.

She eats behind the register while Mr. Josh checks on all the displays. When he's done, he comes up to the register and says, "Mary Beth, I could fire you for eating out here."

Mary Beth keeps right on eating. Mr. Josh walks over to her, and at first, I think he's going to slap her but then it looks like he's going to touch her boob. He removes her nametag. He says, "I'm done playing games."

Mary Beth says she's pregnant, and he says, "Prove it." She pulls her shirt up, revealing her stomach and her bra. I want to tell her that you don't show for almost four months. But Mr. Josh looks at her belly like he can see right through it, into the baby.

Right then, the bells on the door ring, and a man walks in. He walks back to the beer section. From behind, I could swear it's Dylan Rosko. I check the parking lot for a Toyota Tercel. Then, Mary Beth is clinging to my back, crying on my back. I turn around and hug her. Mr. Josh is gone. I tell Mary Beth that it'll be okay, but I know it won't. I know that she will try to mother this child and it just won't work. He'll have bad dreams. Her grandmother will kick her out. Her mother will die.

I hear the bells on the door again. The man walking away—and with beer that he didn't pay for. I look harder, but I can't tell if it's Dylan. If it was, what did he think when he saw me?

When I get home, I can't sleep. So, I stay up watching some television. I think about calling Dylan, and I think about Betton calling to tell us that my mother has died. I ponder these things while watching a show about stars, about how most are dead and the light that we see is dead.

Grandma comes into the room. She still can't sleep until she knows I made it home okay, even if it means she has to wake up at one in the morning to check. This may be why I choose to work the night shift, so that she can sleep. Grandma asks me if Mary Beth liked the meatballs, and I tell her that I think Mary Beth is pregnant.

Jake comes into the living room. He's had another dream.

"Tell me," Grandma says.

And Jake tells her all about his goblins, the strange colors they are and how he knows them but can't remember how or why. He tells her about how they hate her new lipstick and her new smell.

"I'll tell you about goblins," Grandma says. "They're demons, you know. Goblins are demons. But all demons aren't bad. Some of them are like thunderstorms, scaring us straight. Some of them are from the devil, and they want to mislead us. But the devil doesn't take anything away from us. God takes things away from us. Have you read Job at church yet?" Jake shakes his head. "Well, the goblins are trying to take you, but you shouldn't be scared because they're of God and not the devil."

"Where do they want to take me?"

"They won't take you to God," she says. "It's someplace between heaven and hell. You could play all day there. But the problem is that no one there will love you."

"Why can't I play all day here?"

"Because you have to be of the world to be loved by people in the world."

"But we love Jesus, right?" he asks.

"We do, but he doesn't need our love. He wants us to love each other."

Jake seems satisfied with this. "I'm going back to bed. I'll tell them what you said."

We laugh at this once he's out of the room. I think he knows that he can't run away.

Grandma says, "I'm glad for all of your mistakes."

I smile and say, "I hope he can sleep better after this." But I doubt it. Grandma's stories are scary, though not intended to scare. She's Old Testament.

Grandma turns in, and I sit to write Dylan an e-mail. I practice, write it out by hand. I never was good at typing. I write slowly, taking an hour to write some rambling piece of garbage. I won't send this letter. He'll think I'm dumber than he remembers. I want him to remember me well, to think I'm better now than ever. I am. I remember once he told me to fill up my skin with pride. Dylan always liked strength.

Here is a picture for Dylan. Jake before he was Jake. A black and white blob with the almost-shape of a catfish. He's smiling, and there's a glint of purple tracing behind him.

A picture of my mother from a few years back. There is a large building, covered with green ivy. An arbor off the side, which can barely be seen through the pine trees. The lawn, immaculately manicured.

My mother sits in a room, cement blocks for walls. Lunchroom tiles for the floor. A drywall ceiling with one light fixture hanging down. There are two beds in the room, but one is empty. My mother sits on the other, and she stares out of the five-by-three window, stares out at the endless pines in the back. As I approach, she turns to me and I hug her. We don't kiss. She is never the mother that kisses me. Instead, we grapple at each other's shoulder blades. There is something intimate in that. Shoulder blades tell you when someone is happy or sad or sick or dying. My mother's now tell me that she is about to die.

I ask her if she's doing okay. She says, "Those pine trees will be a bitch to deal with in the fall. The needles actually do fall off. Did you know?"

Behind her are pictures that she's drawn, like a child. Scrawling and nonsensical colors. She is like a child with all this medicine that they've given her for what is not her fault, just a disease. I don't believe it. I hug her again, grapple at her shoulder blades, wanting to pull, pull hard—at a wishbone to make a wish.

Jake comes charging into the room. "I did it," he says. "I got them to leave me alone. They chased me, but I won. I got away. The purple one almost caught me."

"So, they're gone now?"

"Yes, the purple one was the saddest to lose me. He said that he'd had plans for us to play tag in a big valley filled with tall grass and lilies and butterflies. He said we'd have so much fun. But I told him I was too old for all that. I told him about you and Grandma and how we all needed each other."

"Did he believe you?"

"He cried, I think, but he was so far behind me that I could only hear him and he was wailing like a baby. He says he'll miss me."

Then, he climbs into my lap. He lays his head on my chest and starts to fall asleep in my arms. He's too old for this. My mother is too young. I will wait for both of them. Perhaps my mother will wake up and Jake will sleep.

I remember the story Grandma told me about demons, or goblins, or whatever she wants to call them. She told me that they would come for me if my parents loved me too much. She told me that the demons were jealous. She said that if they came for me and my parents weren't there, I was to cry, frown, act weak and pathetic. She said if I did that, they wouldn't want me anymore. They would leave me alone.

But we are hard and hungry. We have proven it so. We are thick as locusts. We will stay close to the wall, to the earth, to the food. We will not float away. We will try not to float away.

Jake lifts his sleepy head and asks if he can go swimming. I tell him it's cold outside, and he laughs at me. It's never cold outside here. We are outside quickly. I fill up the kiddie pool, the water hitting the plastic with a sound too loud for nighttime. Jake runs around. I tell him this: "No running around the pool. It's dangerous." I'm joking. This isn't a pool surrounded by slippery cement. Just brown grass.

He laughs again. He strips down to his underwear and looks at me, waiting for me to disapprove. But I'm the too-young mom, the one who never knows how to "establish boundaries." For once, we're together—young. He gets in the pool, and I sit in the pool, my shorts getting soaking wet and freaking cold. I say "fuck" in front of him for the first time. He asks what that means. I say, "That's how you got here, dear heart." He says I should stop talking like Grandma. Through the fence, I see a shadow, a full-grown something moving to and fro, keeping an eye on us. I hear someone crack open a beer. Is it Dylan? I laugh to show how strong I am. The moon above the broken fence. Jake splashes water on me. I get out of the pool and splash water on him. He gets out and splashes water on me. Then, we run around, chasing each other. The dry grass beneath our feet. The dry grass talks, and it says that we will never be okay but we'll be left alone. The old will die off. We will kiss them goodbye. The water on my face. We don't want to die. The dead-of-night moon shines down, and now there is no sound at all. Just light.

In Perfect English

Minutes ago, the mother began cooking. The kitchen is already filled with an eclectic odor, sharp and sweet at the same time, though the smell of eggplant dominates. In a short while, she will finish the dessert. She began the dessert days ago. Almonds, boiled and peeled by hand, lay drying in the laundry room. Odd to begin with the end of the meal, but the end is the best part, where everything makes sense.

The mother has been watching her children, one boy and one girl, Sami and Azar, since the day each came out of her body—and each did so quickly, like lightning from a cloud. They struck her down. She hadn't been able to touch them at first because of fear or, as the doctors said, numbness. She didn't see much of a difference between fear and numbness; one was the cause, the other the effect. Regardless, in the beginning, she could only look. Not until much later did love accompany the watching, but she will never tell because a mother is supposed to love from the beginning. The secret allows her to be a proper mother.

The children are out on the porch, which is green like a wine bottle, long like a ship. There is an old practice of putting ships in bottles. Should she bind her children thus? Always there but always ready to leave. It's hard to know where the fragility lies: in wood or glass, in stillness or motion. Will it be home or the outside world that kills them?

They're outside so her son can smoke. She wishes he wouldn't but is glad the children are home. They come back rarely, and she cannot recall the last time she cooked for someone other than her husband. He is sleeping upstairs. He doesn't eat enough.

But the children, since leaving home, have developed appetites twice as large as the ones they left with. They return ravenous, and she cannot decide if their hunger emerges from a lack of sustenance or insatiability. Regardless, she will feed them. Nourishment is what children should receive at home. They return to remember that they should not starve, that she will not let them.

Looking out, she sees them talking. They were always such talkative children, mouths running from the rising of the sun to the rising of the moon and then sometimes in the dark of night from the secret hallways of their dreams. Always expressing themselves. It makes her proud because she still, after decades, cannot speak English well enough to properly tell a story or relay an emotion. Love. Loneliness. Touching. Touchy. Her children forget everything she says.

Now, she mixes rice, beef, and other things to begin making *dolmeh barg mow*. Hair falls in her face as she wraps grape leaves around rice and beef. Fresh tarragon is required for the dish, but she doesn't have it. Next time they drive into Los Angeles, she'll get some. For the moment, she'll manage. And, yes, soon, she forgets the missing ingredient. She thinks of nothing but the preparation. It is all movement and life as she wraps food with food.

What are the stories that her children tell each other in the light that drips through the leaves above the porch? If she asks, they will tell her, "Oh, nothing. I don't know." They can't even remember their own stories.

ๆ๛

The grape leaves are baking. She has stirred everything, turned some burners off and currently sits at the old kitchen table, the one she cried at when her own mother died. For political reasons, she hadn't been able to go home for the funeral. In that land far away, her sisters and brothers buried their mother below the heat. Her mother forced to slink worm-like into the defiantly cool ground, never to return.

The husband upstairs, silent.

The mother goes into the laundry room to get the almonds. They weren't the best. Almonds from aisle 5 of the American grocery store. She'd noticed their lack of smell as she peeled them for the dessert, *lozeh badam*. She removes the sugar water from the burner to let it cool, and then she mixes almonds, sugar, and cardamom in the blender. The whirring motor sings her happiness.

Then, she combines the finely ground almond mixture with the cooled syrup and begins molding them into shape, the mixture just loose enough not to stick to her hands, just right. She thinks of watching her own mother do this in a place very distant, a place of heat, a town called Nayriz in the middle of many mountains.

She has two different pots of *kateh* going, one for the *fesenjaan* and one for the *ghormeh sabzi*, which are, respectively, Azar's and Sami's favorites. Or at least they used to be. Too many times has she prepared a favorite dish to discover it wasn't at all a child's favorite. Though it saddened her, she tried to rejoice in the fact that they were expressing themselves. Now, she has written down what their favorites are so that she'll never forget.

The smell of eggplant reminds the mother to stir the stew. *Khoresh bademjahn* is her husband's favorite. He should be awake in a few minutes. He'll come downstairs asking only about dinner, not about the children. Sometimes she thinks he is glad that they never come home, though she doesn't understand why because their life is slow and silent without them.

The mother still cannot believe that her children have returned. It's been two years. She's gone to visit each a few times, never for more than two days, and they went on with their lives while she remained in their apartments and cleaned. They wouldn't let her cook for them, said they didn't want a mess in the kitchen. This is one way in which they are alike—and there are so few. She loves them both equally, though she knows their hearts are very different. One will give and one will ask. One will love, the other pierce a nose. Both will leave and never come back, except for food and talk on a chilly night. She puts the *lozeh badam* in the fridge to solidify.

The dessert is done, the sweet mixture cooled. The treats look like stars. When she was younger, her own mother used to tell her not to eat too many because eating stars, like wishing on them, was dangerous. Her children had never made such a connection. They have always called the dessert simply "sweet stuff."

Steam leaks from the pots of rice and rises. The mother follows it with old green eyes. A white mist that could fill your belly rising from the pot to her face to the ceiling, then circling around the room like an amateur belly-dancer. The border in the room is yellow. Yellow ducks—the kind that belong in bathtubs—swimming in a two-dimensional sea. Her children told her years ago that such a border belonged in a bathroom, not in a kitchen. But there it was, out of place, even turning brown with age. The ducks never got anywhere but never stopped swimming. Yelling outside. They can't be fighting. Not now. The food is almost ready. With her hand on the screen door, she is a moment away from yelling to them. *Come in, it's time.* But she hears something boiling over and returns to the stove.

As she reaches for the boiling pot, she stops. She cannot move any more, for there is a hot pain in her that stills her. The floor rises to meet her. She recalls a song about the road rising to meet you. They sang it at both her children's high school graduations. And may the wind blow softly. Outside, she can see the wind evidenced in the trees. She can feel the coolness it brings. All in all, it's been the kind of day that makes one want to stand upon a grassy knoll and look down.

Look down.

(She is always watching.)

Look down.

Yes, there it is. She can see it now. The city. Her children are waiting for her. Everything shines. She sees a city filled with flowers, another filled with heat. From her vantage point, the two can be seen together, *are* together. Then, brighter, white, gone. Darkness and tunnel. There is supposed to be a light at the end of the tunnel.

The trees outside turn into grass. She is, at the same time, looking down on rolling fields and up at thrashing branches. She wonders why they can't hear her but realizes it is because she utters no sound. Used to be able to sing like a nightingale. She sang the story of lovers who lost and found each other. An old story that is told again and again under different titles. If she could use her voice right now, she would sing the tale in perfect English to the children in a voice that would lilt and transcend the wind. The lovers would not be allowed to remain lost.

Exact Warmth

We two live alone here, in relative peace in the big, wide South. But every four months, on average, my daughter Liza suffers a bout of vomiting. Always in the middle of the night. Usually, after a short while, she only dry-heaves, though sometimes she will do so for hours. In these longer sessions, I've been deceived into believing she expelled even when she did not, that abstractions, like food, could be regurgitated. On such nights, presented only with the sound of retching, deep and hollow in the absence of substance, I would think, *Yes, that is her longing for her mother.* Or, *That is her hatred of me.* Or, *That is the impact of stars, misaligned.*

At two o'clock this morning, she wakes me. From the smell of it, she has already thrown up once. Seeing I am awake, she runs back to the bathroom and vomits again. I follow her and try to remember what we had for dinner. I am too tired. Doesn't matter anyway. She pauses, breathes deeply, and begins dry-heaving. I attempt to coax her back to bed. She refuses to leave the bathroom.

A few minutes pass, both of us kneeling on the floor, me halfway holding her so she can break free easily if the bile rises again.

Liza claims our toilet smells like a swimming pool, then climbs into the bathtub and falls asleep clinging to the shower curtain as if it were her mother's hair. She will remain there till morning. This, too, is standard. Liza says the coolness calms her, forces her eyes shut and brings dreams.

A few months ago, I told my mother about these nights. She became distressed, thought I should take Liza to a psychologist.

"Nervous habit," I told her.

"Doug," she said. "There may really be something wrong with her."

She emphasized *wrong*, like the concept was frightening. It's just broad. And that's the problem I have with psychologists. My little girl should only be dealt with in detail.

Right now, for example, I can see how she's grown. Even with her head slightly bowed against the far end of the tub, her feet touch the other end. Water from the faucet drips on her toes, and they twitch in response until she drifts off.

At breakfast, Liza exudes wellbeing, her calm exterior giving lie to a night spent in the bathtub. She rambles about the growth and production in her ant colony.

Liza believes in ants, not in their existence but in their holiness. She trusts them, she claims, because they are too small to deceive. *Where would they hide anything?* she asks. Most kids have favorite animals, but very few have favorite insects. Ants possess powers of stealth that unnerve me. About two years ago, they began to filter upwards through the cracks between the floorboards in our home. When I looked for the insecticide spray, I discovered Liza had disposed of it. I bought more, but she fell into a fit as I began to use it. To make up for my murderous acts, I bought and set up an ant farm for Liza. She's been a loving and dedicated caretaker to them for well over a year now.

Hopefully, Liza will soon become distracted. Her favors and alliances shift. It's come to my attention that there is a new species of monkey in Bolivia and a contest to name the creature sponsored by Animal Aid. The new monkey alone wouldn't be enough. The contest—well, Liza loves a challenge. In the center of the table, I've displayed the newspaper article about the new monkey.

"There are romances budding all over the place," she exclaims, referring to her ant colony. "Unless they're fighting. I think it's mating because no one dies."

"Liza, will you hand me the salt?" I ask, encouraging her discovery of the newspaper.

"But it's all the way across the table," she says. "You're closer."

"Please," I beg.

She shifts onto her knees, then rises in her chair to reach the salt. She pauses, mid-reach, upon finding a furry monkey with mournful eyes staring up at her. Liza forgets the salt altogether and begins to pet the picture. In a moment, she is sitting on the table, looking at the newspaper.

"Daddy, did you see this?" Liza asks.

"Sure," I say, casually. "They just want your money, you know."

There is a fee for entering the contest, a donation of sorts, but Liza gasps, offended.

"Are they selling him?" she asks. Though her animal activism is currently tied up in ants, Liza extends her ideology to all creatures. I wonder why she doesn't see her ant colony for the prison it is. For the moment, I clear the breakfast dishes and sit in the chair below my daughter. I place my hands on her knees, noting their diminishing angularity, and tell her of the new monkey in Bolivia that we will save by naming.

Liza's hair brushes the table. It is longer than it has ever been. When she was younger, we never had to cut it. Then, she turned eight and a mane grew in. Though naturally wavy, almost curly, the length straightens her hair. A few strands manage to retain wave, causing the texture to be uneven. It hasn't been cut for six months and now threatens to sweep the floor. A Clydesdale horse joins the family. She gallops off.

I go to the kitchen window and place my hand against the
pane, chilly to the touch. The first truly cool day of this Southern
fall, a day with a difference that causes you to notice and
remember. The day itself cannot be enjoyed, haunted by a
general sense of deja vu that, if explored, leads to memory
upon memory. Most recent of these: Cathy planting tulips.
Whenever she became confused, which seemed to occur more
frequently in the fall, Cathy turned to garden upkeep. I suppose
she relished the proof of primed soil, dead weeds, flowers in
earthen pots, plants in the earth. I never understood her affinity
for tulips, though. Tulips are vague. They go into the ground
and return months later according to no precise schedule. Or
maybe the tulips are on a schedule and I should instead blame
the erratic Southern weather. Some years, we skip right over
spring. In one April-summer, Cathy had easily forgotten to
expect tulips, and the surprise caused her to sit on the grass in
the yard and cry. This jarred me. All she would say through her
sobs was *I love remembering like this.*

Liza spends all afternoon in her room drawing pictures of the
monkey. "I have to know him before I can give him a name,"
she says. Somehow being able to reproduce visual features, short
hairs and dark eyes, warrants that intimacy.

I travel the house, staring at the floorboards for any
movement. My life is like that: boring from a distance, frightening
up close. You often don't know the ants are there until you
bring your face within inches of the floor and a rouge ant jumps
onto your nose. So, don't get too close. Stay there, where the
floor looks like a floor.

Evening settles like the tail end of a breeze. I've relinquished
my quest for insects, deciding that, for today at least, the only
ones visible are enclosed by glass. Ants are more prone to move
near or into houses in cold temperatures. They forage less. Their
actual food preferences change, too, or so claims my neighbor.

He recommends bait in the summer—one that contains spinosad, which is less toxic and safer for kids—and individual mound treatments in the winter. I prefer to stay inside, though, away from the concentrated domain of danger. I will keep Liza in here with me. She will be satisfied to have a little bit of the external world under her control. Despite Liza's peaks of compulsion, she accomplishes incredible calm most of the time.

My wife Cathy was never so easily at peace. She left me once for a few weeks. It led me to believe that I was the cause of her despair. Another fall memory.

She had just come in from gardening. Her face darker than it actually was, fair skin bronzed with dust. "I'm tired," she said. "I'm going to Greenville."

"What is it that's so tiring?" My voice remained level, calm, so she could not discern any anger. Her sister, who had been unjustly suspicious of my stoic nature, lived in Greenville. She had other friends that lived just as close that she could stay with. The declaration of a visit to her sister's was actually the answer to my question. But Cathy said, "You. And Liza."

Then, she left. She didn't say how long she would be away, and I wasn't sure if I should be alarmed. I recall my pain in wondering if she would return, in missing her. Now, she is dead, and I have nothing to wonder. I've supposed a million times that this is why I do not miss her, the lack of uncertainty, the lack of possibility. I remember her, sure, though without longing for her. My memories will fade. In time, I will forget her eyes, their color and movement in light.

Tulips come from Holland. There, the flowers roam free in wooden clogs—the desire to hear their own footsteps satisfied. Tulips are certain of their presence.

Our weather in the Upstate is a bit more regular than the rest of the state, meaning that in winter it's more likely to stay cold. *Probably because of the mountains*, says my neighbor. *A brisk wind, ever now and then, brings the senses back to life. It's the difference,* he claims. He means to say *every* instead of ever and *contrast* instead of difference. This is why I stay inside—because it becomes tiresome interpreting. Eventually, imprecision will drive me from the South.

I've always been allotted a small space in the living room, a corner, for my bookcases and an armchair in which to read. That is where Liza finds me.

"What's for dinner?" she asks, still hyper from an afternoon of basking in novelty. It's not often a child gets to name an entire species.

"I haven't really thought of dinner," I say.

"I thought of a name." Liza pauses, leans heavily on the arm of my chair. "Wachuchu."

"Wachuchu," I repeat. "I like it. How'd you come up with it?

"Not sure exactly," she begins, but I can see she's going to give me the run-down. "It's a small monkey. Two pounds. And I like the sounds. Wa. Chu. Like sneezing, you know?" Liza climbs on the arm and sits there, perfectly balanced on her knees. She leans in a little, then back, just to show off. The next lean forward, however, throws off her balance and she falls forward. I catch her before her face hits the opposite arm. "You're too old to be messing around like this."

"Yeah," she breathes, revealing her shock and perhaps some shame.

Then, she turns over so that I'm cradling her like I did so often when she was younger. Does she remember? Do those sleepless nights when I rocked her and sang her my lullaby adaptations of classic rock songs still occupy a part of her consciousness? Can she recall the third birthday party where I dressed up as a llama and took all of her friends for rides? I even made sure to spit for comic effect—and it's harder than you think to spit when expected to. I have never been stoic with Liza, yet perhaps I must do more. I often suspect that the actions of the father are downplayed or forgotten because they are considered duties. The role of the mother is a calling, not a duty, and it is assumed that everything she does she is compelled rather than expected to do. I, too, am compelled to nurture, love, protect. To understand. Fatherhood is not an emotional superlative. I will prove this to my daughter. It will be my gift to her.

"Can we have brownies for dinner?" Liza asks.

Her hair feels like turf, and I cringe to realize she hasn't showered since vomiting. She promises to wash it—right now, too—if we can have brownies for dinner.

When Liza returns, I see that she has cut her hair in addition to washing it. So that she won't have to wash her hair as often, she says. It is neater short, so I should like it. But I don't. The act seems self-destructive to me. She denies growth—even if it is only one kind.

She actually resembles a monkey now. Wachuchu is jealous. He puffs out the orange tuffs on either side of his face by inflating his cheeks. He is the winner by a small, colorful margin.

"Do you like my new haircut?" Liza asks me, providing her own version of a runway walk in which she juts out her midsection so far that I fear she will fall backwards.

Wachuchu laughs maniacally, dances between her feet as she steps to and fro, taking sharp model turns. I watch closely, gauging the magic and potential danger. Wachuchu is just as Liza described him, just as his name describes him. He is wet, too, from showering. I send them both off to dry their hair.

I rummage through a box of letters I keep on the bottom shelf of one of my bookcases. It contains pictures of Cathy and the best letters I ever wrote to her. I initially intended to spend more time with the pictures, to exercise my remembrance. But I've found the letters more appealing. I like to reread them. It reminds me that I am powerful, which I forget often in the midst of this banality. And even though these letters were once part of the day-to-day, they are more than that now. More even than nostalgic. They contain mantras. *I will see you soon, in August when summer will wrap us tight in its wet blanket. I sensed you last night, a finger digging in my unclean navel.*

Liza returns with Wachuchu wrapped around her neck. "Do you still love her?" she asks. "You seem to in those."

"You've read these?" I ask, feeling angrier than I should.

"Some. They're right there on the bottom shelf."

I grab her hand, and shaking my head say, "Don't do that again." I haven't employed this gesture since she was five or six, but I'm familiar with it, and the familiarity undercuts the lack of control I sense.

"I won't," she says, sounding trustworthy yet subtly slipping her hand out of my grip.

On the top of the pile in the box, I find a postcard of a tree-lined street in Savannah. I can't recall what took me there. On the back, I wrote, *This southern beauty is no substitute for you.*

Liza takes the postcard from me, asks, "What's southern beauty?"

I turn it around to show her the photograph on the front.

"A street?"

"No, here," I say, tracing a beam of light from sky to Spanish moss to cobblestone street.

And she looks more closely, eager to see the surrogate beauty.

After Liza is asleep, Wachuchu and I step out for a cigarette. I can still smell the upturned earth, despite the evening chill. Cathy's gardening gloves lie on the porch railing. They are old winter gloves, not truly gardening gloves. I practice remembering Cathy. The amount of fat on her calves and her thighs, which I always grabbed because I could find none around her waist. The fine hairs on the back of her neck, the thicker ones on her forearms. The curls in her hair, much tighter than Liza's. And the exact warmth, to the degree, of her breath on my neck. The recollections provide the smallest assurance.

Wachuchu reminds me I quit smoking long ago.

Yes, I tell him, but after a night of Liza vomiting, I needed one. I won't fall into the habit again. He doesn't seem to believe me. He wanders toward the flowerbed and begins sniffing. He places a pinch of dirt in his mouth and then stares upwards at the moon in contemplation.

In the furthest point of the yard by the fence where there are no streetlights, some creature makes a sound. A heavy creature. Wachuchu claims he can tell. He has that fight-or-flight instinct. After sniffing the air delicately, the way Cathy did right after she'd applied perfume, he declares it is a predator. And though I say we have no predators, I believe him because the tufts of orange stick straight out. The foreboding, I'm sure, will keep us both awake, regardless of its truth.

Wachuchu has corrected me. Tulips are from Turkey.

We are asleep on the couch when we hear Liza vomiting. Around two o'clock. I find her in the bathtub, except this time it appears she has been throwing up in the tub rather than into the toilet. The puke isn't draining and the small puddle reaches her bare feet, only inches from the drain.

"Liza," I whisper, as I lift her. I hold her gently, securely, and rub her back.

"Put me back!" she yells.

I place her on the counter and wash her feet in the sink. She leans over and vomits again onto her feet. I leave the water running and start the water running in the tub as well, using the showerhead to clear the mess. Behind me, Liza quiets down, falls into low moans. I return to her and finish rinsing her feet, then clear the sink. I coax her to rinse her mouth. She leans over the sink to do so but begins dry heaving again. In the small mess that she forces out, I spot redness. It could be spaghetti sauce from dinner. I dip my finger in and smell this redness, like the detectives on crime shows. I cannot discern anything but the rancid stink of vomit. I yearn to call my mother, but I am ashamed and afraid. Wachuchu, sensibly, yells from the hallway that we must take Liza to the emergency room.

Outside the hospital in the parking lot, they are doing roadwork. In the back of a truck containing stacks of orange cones, a man sits with his head propped up on his fist, looking studious. As I approach, I can tell he is asleep. The deceiving image of this man causes me to doubt the weight of Liza in my arms. I shift to make sure that I have a strong grip, that we are both here. She coughs again, and I rush toward the door. The smell of demolished asphalt fills my nostrils, protecting them from the hospital's stereotypical aromas. I am grateful.

Once they are ready to see Liza, she has stopped throwing up. I brought a bag, which she had to use twice. I discarded it in a trashcan, though I'm not sure if that's the right place for it. The doctor arrives and gives Liza a once-over, takes her temperature and checks her pulse.

"What seems to be the problem tonight?" he asks. The doctor is a short man with a narrow face and a nose that is too wide. It's the kind of distinct face comic books attribute to bad guys. Cathy would have said he looked *nice*, reminded her of her father. Or something like that.

"She's been throwing up repeatedly," I say.

He returns his gaze to Liza and checks her eyes with a penlight. "Did she eat anything she might be allergic to?"

"She's not allergic to anything."

"Were her meals prepared in a restaurant or at home?"

"Home."

"Did you eat the same things she did?"

"Yes."

"Think now," he insists. "Anything she ate that you didn't?"

"No, we ate exactly the same meals at the same time."

He grunts, I cannot tell if in confusion or disbelief. "What did you eat?"

"We had eggs and pancakes for breakfast, spaghetti for lunch, and later brownies."

"So, no dinner?"

"The brownies."

"For dinner?" He sighs, saying, "That might be it."

"No, this happens all the time. Every four months or so, she has a vomiting fit. Usually, it's just one night. But she got sick yesterday, too."

"Is this the first time you've taken her to a doctor?"

"She's been to our GP," I say. "He said she just had a sensitive stomach."

"Liza," the doctor says. "Did you eat anything your daddy didn't see you eat today?"

She shakes her head. He continues staring to make sure this is the extent of her response.

"Can I talk to you outside, sir?" the doctor asks.

Once in the hallway, he tells me he is hooking Liza up to an I.V. for fluids, and then he is going to take blood and urine samples. The repetition of Liza's condition concerns him, so he is also going to have the hospital psychologist come to talk to her first thing in the morning.

"Is your wife here?" the doctor asks.

"No, she's dead."

He nods slightly. I'm unable to decipher his intention. "Your daughter's sickness may be an expression of grief."

"It's been four years."

"Sometimes it just takes that long," he says, softly and slowly.

I return to Liza and find her asleep. There is nothing for me to do. Wachuchu tells me to go get a drink. He will watch Liza. I tell him he has no parental instincts.

As I sit in a chair by her bed, I try to recall what psychological trauma she might have been exposed to. Liza was too young to be affected by Cathy's death. And the possibility of inheritance is slight. Cathy was always manic. When I first met her almost fifteen years ago, we were both freshman in Charleston. But she, unlike all of the college students, did not have an aura of youth about her. She was not an old soul or ethereal. Cathy was simply impatient. She shed youth because she would have to do it anyway. Clean sweeps. That is what drew me in, though not what kept me with her. How can I tell you about that other thing? Wachuchu shrugs and points to a sexy nurse standing at the foot of the bed next to Liza's. But it is not that and more than that.

The hospital psychologist says Liza may have an anxiety disorder and gives me the number of a psychologist in private practice. The E.R. doctor himself has nothing more to add about Liza's condition, says he will call if any of the tests come back with unusual findings. The calmness of both men is comforting to me, but Wachuchu glares distrustingly from the bed. He didn't sleep at all. I gather Liza in my arms and leave. She is slightly awake. Wachuchu jumps onto my shoulder and begins to make faces at her so she will laugh. I don't think Liza can see him at all, though. He would love her anyway.

We all three squint at the morning, dim as it is yet. The road crew is gone. The orange cones remain, arranged in a line at the opposite side of the parking lot. Sensing kinship, Wachuchu wants to play there amongst them.

As I place Liza into her own bed, she tells me to feed her ants. I'm not really sure how to do this, but I agree. She falls asleep easily then.

Wachuchu reminds me that I must call in our name for him so we can all be rich. The contest deadline is today.

Downstairs, I call Animal Aid and am connected with a customer service representative.

"I'd like to enter a name in the Bolivian monkey contest," I say.

"Sir," she responds, sounding very well rehearsed, "it isn't a contest. It's an auction. If you look at the information again, you'll see this described in detail."

"Okay, then I'd like to place a bid on a name."

"Very well," she says. "How will you be securing your bid?"

"With a credit card."

She takes some general information and my card number. We are closing the deal, and I'm certain that our name will win. Liza will awaken to a victory.

"Wonderful," the representative replies. "The high bid is six hundred thousand five."

I hang up, pulling my hand back quickly as if quickness could undo the trouble. Wachuchu turns with a questioning glance. I tell him nothing, lest he disappear into his own disappointment.

Ants will eat tulips, you know. The oiliness of stalks appeals to them. But only in summer. I dream of mutilated stalks dissipating into a swarm of ants. The blossom itself falls to the earth where it is left untouched.

After taking a nap, I check the cabinets and fridge for something Liza can eat later, and I see that we need milk. Since cereal should be an option and brownies may later be required for recovery, Wachuchu and I drive to the store. He settles on my right shoulder and remains quiet, except when I turn left and the momentum threatens to throw him off entirely. Then, he squawks, just briefly, like a mockingbird.

The grocery store's parking lot is crowded, and on the long walk to the storefront, other customers stare at Wachuchu. He moves through embarrassment, delight, and anger. He hides, he peeks, he stares back aggressively. I'm the owner of a schizophrenic monkey.

Just as we approach the doors, several people run toward us yelling. All I can make out is "God," or maybe "Go." Wachuchu motions that we should proceed. However, he isn't the best judge of human behavior. He probably perceives *terrified* as *happy* or something. Or maybe he just likes trouble. There's no telling with him. Wachuchu keeps his motivations to himself.

I hold back, moving under the shelter of a shopping-cart-return station. After a few minutes, two men silently rush out of the store. They look a little scared, mostly in a hurry. The taller man unlocks a blue, 1970s Chevy Nova. As the other man places his hand on the passenger door handle, he turns to survey the parking lot and spots me leaning against a metal pole next to almost twenty shopping carts. He yells, "Hey!" Wachuchu answers with a double-squawk, sounding more like the monkey he is. We are not afraid. The man starts toward us, though, our bravery irrelevant. But his friend barks at him, and he backs away. Wachuchu is disappointed. I'm annoyed because we must drive to another store for the milk.

The front door is cracked open when we return. I walk in, call out, "Liza?" There is no answer. Nervously, Wachuchu and I mount the stairs. In Liza's room, we find an empty bed and an empty closet. I scan the room for a note, but there is none. Cathy never wrote me either. I spot Liza's overturned ant farm. Spilt sand transforms the vacant room into a messy, mid-summer boardwalk. Wachuchu brushes at his arms and climbs onto me for refuge. It's no use. The ants, captive and wild, are all over me, too. They don't bite as I expect. Instead, my skin feels hot. Liza isn't really gone. Little pieces of her are still here, slithering with the energy she gave them. This was her intention all along. *My daughter is an ant.* I whisper it once, twice, and I find that with the mantra I remember that other thing about Cathy. Wachuchu squeals and claims this isn't the time. But I stand still, close my eyes, and tell him about tulips. Then, my body is devoured, and my head falls to the floor.

You Who Have Eyes

Nighttime, like usual. Mom is done with dinner, but it still smells like she's cooking those too-spicy tacos, acidic with cumin. I watch her cook. She doesn't know how to use the stove fan, which would suck those tacos up to the moon, melt their cold silver cheese. The tacos always mess up my stomach, but Mom says I'm too young to have stomach problems and makes them anyway.

Daddy is home, and straight into their bedroom. And speaking of coldness, when I go in to see if he wants ice cream for dessert, he looks up at me from underneath the crook of his elbow. But his eyes are only there for a second and then, like a lizard catching the sense of my heat, they're quickly gone away into the early darkness. Movement in the corner of my own eyes. Maybe that's all a daddy should be. There's no answer, which means more dessert for me.

In the living room, Mom holds her empty dessert bowl and watches *Wheel of Fortune*. Except she doesn't call out the answers, like most adults. Her eyes are empty, too, but the difference is, Daddy's at least move. For Mom, there are no secrets here, none in those letters. She won't cry out for nothing. Maybe she already knows the answers.

I've been working hard all week at school, learning something about multiplication and rhyme. It's hard to remember all of it, especially on a full stomach.

For a little while, I lie on the couch and watch the *Wheel*, feeling nauseous. Then, I get it: *All for love, the world well lost.* There was a play, and my older sister was in it. Mom said Cleopatra surely could have been black. Why not? And I am yelling like a banshee, despite a twist-and-turn stomach and all of our exhaustion.

The morning is hazy, and I stay inside till I can see the sun. Our apartment complex doesn't have a playground, so we just roam until ideas strike. Sometimes we'll roll down a slope, and other times, we'll throw little rocks at a window to drive that orange cat nuts. Most often, we play on the gate that separates the back end of our apartment complex from the neighborhood on the other side. A "Dead End" sign isn't enough. I guess there wouldn't be a dead end if the gate wasn't here, the road running all the way through like it does.

This four-foot gate, it goes all the way across the road, and they only open it on trash day for the trucks. My friend Cyrus can hang upside down on it without his hands touching the pavement. He's six and still short and small like that. In the house just on the other side, there's an old lady. She's just about blind, I think, because people are always leading her here and there. She should get one of those sticks. Or a dog. I mean, her husband works all day. It doesn't seem right. We like her because she's always out in the yard where we can spy on her.

I join Cyrus hanging on the Dead End gate and ask him where the blind lady and her husband are. He says, "They left earlier. You'd been out here, you'd know they were gone."

"I'm not coming to sit outside if it's cloudy like rain is coming," I say.

We sit quietly for a moment, and then Cyrus flips right-side up and hops to the ground to stand behind me and run his hands through my hair. Sometimes, he'll do rough braids for me. My mom always complains about the mess. But I like it when he does my hair. He's young enough and enough years younger than me to play just so without his friends making fun of him for liking a girl.

He stops braiding, and we see a car top off the hill and pull into the driveway too fast, scraping. The blind lady's husband gets out and goes inside. "He must've left her at a store or something," Cyrus says.

I cling to the to gate's bar hard enough to get rust and orange and white paint flecks embedded in the grooves of my palm. While Cyrus unbraids my hair, ready to start over, I pick the trash off my hand, wondering how a psychic would read my future to me. Would it be full of this falling-apart stuff, this vomit smell of old coins' metal?

Cyrus just snagged himself a yellow butterfly, solid with no markings, in one of those bug cages you buy at the store. His mom keeps him equipped. We're sitting on the grass in midday heat, which is worse because the haze is back. So, we're squinting and sweating. And the butterfly reaches through the mesh, tickling my hand, but I'm not ticklish. Cyrus squirms just watching, though.

Then, there's the sound of craziness, too close. The blind lady is back with a couple. They're all running out of the house, onto the front lawn. The blind lady is yelling crazy-jive language. It isn't English. I can tell she's talking nothing in any language, though. It's like that sound you make when you scrape yourself up and your mother isn't anywhere close.

Cyrus says, "Shit," and moves over to the Dead End sign, staying quiet and near the edge to be sort of polite. The blind lady does this tough girl thing, holding back tears by squishing her eyes shut and breathing through her nose. The other woman, the blind lady's sister, I think, holds her, but she's too wide-eyed herself to do a good job.

Then, a siren, too close, coming from just the other side of the Dead End sign. All of our parents come outside. Even my mother. Mothers squeezing us to them and, at first, trying to redirect our gazes, and the fathers crowding around the gate whispering about the yard and yardwork that'll have to be done later, how they'll help. But then we're allowed to be without our parents. This business is nothing new for them. Fourth of July fireworks, the movie's happy ending. Maybe they think it'll do us good to figure out grief and death. Well, death is an ambulance and a noise, a sheet and a woman crying. I'm schooled now.

In the early darkness, Cyrus and I stay outside till everything is quiet as a church at the blind lady's house. Till the sisters have gone. Till Cyrus thought better of it and let the butterfly go.

"We should give her something," he says. And I think he's right. That's what you do when you're afraid and sad at the same time. So, we write her a letter. Well, I do most of it.

Dear Blind Lady,

We're sorry about your husband. I'm sure he loved you and you loved him. My friend Cyrus let his butterfly go.

All for love, the world well lost.

Sincerely,

The Kids from the Apartments

Cyrus runs onto her porch. He leaves a honeysuckle branch in a red picnic cup and the note next to it. We go back to playing. The rain never came, but it smells wet and fresh out here. There is a chill coming in. Cyrus shivers like a new puppy. He's always exaggerating. Cyrus says, "What you think he died of?"

"I don't know," I say. "But I know he died for love."

"You can't know that."

"Sure I can," I say. "He loved her."

"All sorts of ways he could've died," says Cyrus. "Maybe he choked to death."

"He didn't choke."

"I always thought she would die first."

"She won't die," I say.

"My mom said a woman can't live without her man if she loved him."

"Cyrus, that just isn't so."

"That's what she said."

I should tell Cyrus not to believe everything his mother tells him. Would it break his heart? Anyway, every house is different, and no one can see all the way inside a house. Or all the way inside a man or a woman. It might be silly to believe we're all the same. I hope that lady's husband died nice, though I doubt it. I hope she keeps our note forever. I hope she stays warm and tough and doesn't go empty in the eyes.

Forseti in the White City

Odin! Dost thou remember
When we in early days
Blended our blood together?
When to taste beer
Though did'st constantly refuse
Unless to both 'twas offered?[1]

In chi-town, the white city[2], the windy city, the city with the big shoulders[3]. The shoulders that hold up the world, like Atlas, that god. That god whom we all know.

In Haskell Hall, where soon I will be cast out.

When my mother told me to pick a major, I wanted to be a

---

[1] Saemund's Edda, Thorpe's translation. Benjamin Thorpe was the god of the Anglo-Saxon language for a long time, though no god like Forseti! Thorpe was the first to translate the elder Edda. He spent his life immersed in Anglo-Saxon language and poetry, translating. One thing never equaled another. By all accounts, one could say he was obsessed.

[2] Daniel Burnham, the architect who oversaw the construction of the World's Columbian Exposition. He had a partner, J.W. Root, but Root died of pneumonia and Burnham was left in charge. Modern design scrapped. Classic revival. White buildings.

[3] "Chicago" by Carl Sandburg, who wanted to write American fairy tales for his daughters, tales truer than those including kings and queens. Kings and queens of the fairy tales don't exist.

writer, but I decided to be an anthropologist. It is what my brother did before me. He has a tenure-track position at Harvard. He has books published. He is five years my senior, and he asks me, "Joseph, when will you buckle down and get to work?" He fancies himself a success. People call him a success. He acts like he's my father. Perhaps, I worshipped him as such.

I know another god, whom you don't know. His name is Forseti.

Forseti, God of Justice. He wraps his cape around himself and retreats to the fortress of solitude when the nights get cold. No, he isn't a superhero. I don't know what he looked like. There are no busts or statues.

Though a minor Norse god, I've long suspected that Forseti precipitated the fall of all the Norse gods. In the accepted Norse mythological texts, Forseti plays no part in Ragnarok, but I have always believed that the God of Justice must play a role in the end of times, the endgame, the apocalypse.

Was he Clark Kent, unrecognizable as God of Justice?

I have found scraps of documents, documents that no one else finds significant because of the documents' incompleteness. In one, "Forseti is the cause of Ragnarok, the kindness that brought cruelty that brought the end."[4] In another, "Forsete stood aside and cried, but he made no apology for his role in all of this."[5]

The greatest discovered manuscript to date is mine now, paid for in full, flying across the Atlantic. I will translate it. You will see how the story ends.

In Haskell Hall, where I will soon be cast out. A Friday when I should want to leave, but instead, I desire acceptance. The Norns' song changes, though—as sung by three sisters. My fate is and is not sealed. I wait for the Word of my Sister.

---

[4] Brock MS 3464. Sir William Brock bought the manuscript from a shepherd who claimed to have found it buried in a tree.

[5] Graves MS 2187. Graves not likely the name of the person who found the manuscript. This manuscript was passed down for almost one hundred years. The last owner gave it his own name, but there's no way of telling if the manuscript was passed down patrilineally.

On the Michicago committee for scheduling and such, Mrs. Green says, Sorry, we can't accept your proposal on— and she stumbles over his name. *Forseti*, I say. I ask why not. She says, "No one else is really interested in Norse myth anymore. It's been done." I say, "If it's been done, then why don't you know his name?" She rolls away from me in her big office chair.

I stand alone, amongst tile—hard on the floor and soft on the ceiling—and fluorescence and green vinyl chairs. I stand with the secretaries and student workers, some wandering colleagues. Mailboxes. The smell of copy toner mixed with microwave lunches. I stand in the main office. I stand alone amongst them. There is a Dali poster of a butterfly, a big blue butterfly, behind Mrs. Green's desk. On her desk are pictures of children in swimsuits. I like to believe that we all want more than this day-to-day. But these boorish shadows want nothing more than banalities, banalities of family and fame. No one knows what became of art. It no longer exists and, thus, anthropology. They're all clinging to the levee or making millions off Buddy Holly. No one wants to know the story anymore. You don't want to know.

As I return to my office, Claire Richards stops me. She teaches about Senegambia and pirates—not together. She says, "Walk with me." She's the kind of woman who says *walk with me* and then hooks her arm through yours. I tell her about my failure. We've known each other for a few months, and I've sensed her wanting a secret or an intimacy from me. She says, "Don't worry. You can do your presentation on my panel, on comparative mythology." She says, "Just compare your gods to other gods. Look for shared themes, similarities." This sounds very much like equivocation, but I agree. She half-hugs me, and her hair is strawberry blonde and smells of strawberries.

I wanted to be a writer so that I could tell the stories no one is interested in. Yet, these are the most important stories, the stories we have forgotten. I don't know what story I had in mind back then, when I first wanted to write. Now, though, I have one.

Forseti. His mother was Nauna, the moon goddess.

In a house green with envy, two brothers. Our mother was a wise woman. She told us both we were smart and handsome. But our father died before he could tell us more than *I love you*. Did Mother become a lover we were trying to impress? Did Oedipus haunt our home? Perhaps, yet we all remained calm and alive. We all retained our sight.

My brother, however, became a genius. My mother took him to a specialist when he was ten, and the specialist said that his IQ was *off the chart*. Of course, it was off the chart. I have no lust for genius. I envied my mother, how she knew my father. How—I could not remember. When you don't know your father, you want to tell his story. You stand over the small round table with the glass top. You remember your father holding a light underneath, placing your template and blank page on top, and telling you, Here, this is the best way to trace, follow the lines. Now, the table is covered with a white tablecloth, and the house has been painted white, an off-white which your mother calls yellow.

His father was Balder, the god of innocence and purity. He shone immutability. Nauna moved like water, like waves, in Balder's presence.

My brother V. writes me and tells me that he's going to Michicago this year. He always goes. This year, however, I'm going, too, and I'll be on a panel with a strawberry blonde. And I'll be comparing gods.

Dear Joseph,

Will be in Chicago soon, just two months. I'm bringing you some old textbooks that might help you with your research, or rather that might help you get on track with some research that isn't

redundant or obsolete. I will be presenting in
section II: META-HISTORIES OF ETHNIC
AND NATIONAL IDENTITIES. My panel is
called "Where Have All the Local Women Gone?
Language, Practice and the Semeiosis of Variety in
the Historical Bayou." I think Mother would be
proud. My research explains a lot.
   -V.

   My brother does, studies, the same thing over and over, which
many say is the sign of insanity. I have no lust for genius. I will
bear the burden of one story, of telling it all the way through
just once. You just wait.

The snow hasn't thawed yet. I don't know if it will. The sidewalks
speak, and the sky is mute. The buildings stand like anemic
fingers, pointing to nothing, to no salvation. The weather is
worse, colder, this year. Yes, colder. A package from Iceland
arrives. Old text, but no *textbook*. I want to make the myth true,
to make the myth human. If you think this is what Shakespeare
did, you're halfway right. But it's more than that. You must
become part of the story. There is mysticism involved, a
connection. Rumi says, "Who speaks words with my mouth?"[6]
Yes, who?
   This manuscript was discovered, mentioned briefly in
Current Anthropology a few years ago. A manuscript focusing
on Balder, Forseti's father. I contacted the journal and then
the purported discoverer, Jan Steffenson. I asked him for the
document, begged him. Ten years later, after no one else would
believe that his findings were legitimate—something about
inconclusive carbon dating results—he finally sent me the
manuscript. A sort of Eddaic apocrypha, it supposedly (though
inconclusively) predates the *Codex Regius* by at least two

---

[6] "Who Says Words With My Mouth" by Rumi, Coleman Barks's translation. I
   wish to be a Sufi, for the science of God.

hundred years, and it outlines the secrets. Yet, they are only secrets to the discerning eye. To others, the stories are frivolous, inconsequential—a woman combing her hair (strawberry blonde?) or a retelling. I believe these secrets do more than reveal the inconsequential. I think these secrets reveal the extent of the early Christian influence, sure, but more importantly, the minor gods acting in major ways that lead to *peripetia*. Why do we stifle certain figures and not others? The answer is simple: to make the story accessible, a cautionary tale, a thing beyond humanity. Zeus acts like a child? Yes, an absurd god rather than human.

My theory is simply this: the god Forseti, his story is untold. His story is told through others. His story is the beginning and the end. The apocryphal poet says,

> O, Allfather, you opened Ginnunga-gap
> And Nifl-heim and Muspells-heim
> Fire and ice (some say that...)
> And Ymir and Audhumla.
>
> Desperation creates children
> Of all the coldness, and then a fight
> The world began and began again
> Then, the flesh, which will die.[7]

He who knows the beginning is ready for crime and justice. We say, *In the beginning was the word*, and we refer to *the word of the law*. But I say, *He who knows the beginning is ready for justice*. Who truly knows the beginning is simply ready. We must follow things through. The myth of origin is a myth. The ur-myth, our greatest folly. We edit out the specifics so that we may not see the end, so that we may all be together. You must not be alone.

---

[7] Eddaic apocrypha (Steffenson MS 1445). Steffenson found the manuscript himself, not in a tree but in a leather case buried in a peat bog in Ireland—preserved like skin, like a body.

His grandfather is the Great Odin, god of sky and war. Odin rules all of the Aesir, all of the Nine Worlds, still to this day.

In my apartment, the walls are bare. Everything is put away, in its rightful place. Only the dining room table sits untidy, with this Eddaic apocrypha. Shall we eat? I eat soup, and then I translate. The text alternates between prose and verse, and, it seems, is told by Forseti:

"Breidablik, the great hall of my childhood, repels evil with its mirrors. The passageways are lined with mirrors. Freyr blessed our home's paint so that even the exterior shimmers to blind evil. But my family, we are not blinded. When I was a young boy, it was clear to me that the mirrors reflected, nay illuminated, whatever came before them. Stepping slowly alongside the mirrors, I stared at my image. I came to know myself."

A stunning use of first person in the prosaic portions. I know of no other ancient text that does so—no other ancient text that is known or revered, that is. The bravery to tell the story. Of course, to believe in the legitimacy of the text requires belief in gods. You believe, don't you?

I'm up all weekend, save for the early hours of Monday morning. I have lost myself, perhaps, but the story is unfolding. The musky truth lulls me to sleep. I'm gliding down the Thames-Congo on the *Nellie*, telling my story to the setting sun. There was between us the bond of the sea.[8]

The hallways of Haskell are catacombs—Who shall I seal in? A friend, enemy, brother?[9]—yet the bright light. Monday morning: a bleaching grounds, a feat of making white with off-white, with buttermilk. A feat of runes. Claire gives me our schedule. Our panel is in section V. We are scheduled two days after my brother's panel.

---

[8] *Heart of Darkness* by Joseph Conrad, who declined British knighthood.
[9] "The Cask of Amontillado" by Edgar Allan Poe, who died yelling another man's name, perhaps his friend's or his killer's.

I walk down the hallway, drenched in anxiety. My colleagues find me redundant and obsolete. Like my brother, they all study fresh locales—the Middle East and Africa and Asia and the Caribbean and that small town on the bank of the Amazon and forgotten USofA and sites of conflicts and natural disasters. And of course, technology, which makes everything fresh.

"The Meaning of Cute is Very Deep: Gendering Androgyny in Japanese Conversation"

"Generation 'Txt': The Cell Phone and the Crowd in the Contemporary Philippines"

"Who's That Lady?: Ahmadinejad's Veiled Female Posturing"

"Here Comes the Story of the Hurricane: Diametrical National Views of the French Quarter Post-2005"

"Functions of voice quality in a Zapotec region of Oaxaca"

"How the Marshallese Think—About Turtles, Possessives, and Nuclear Weapons, for Instance"

"Stepford Husbands: The Robotics of Middle America"

"The Upside-down Crow's Nest: Foucauldian Dynamics and Mythology on the Seventeenth-Century Pirate Ship"[10]

The title of my presentation will be "Atlas, the Betrayer, and Forseti, the God of Justice." I suppose it sounds like comic books, which I read when I was younger. For lack of physical strength, maybe. My mother always said that superheroes were weak, too, but I told her that was just a pretense. My mother never argued with me. She spoke her piece, and if you disagreed, she walked away. She walked away in beauty. She lived in what seemed to be a world beyond ours, a world where she was protected and not the protector.

His grandmother is Frigg, goddess of motherhood. She possesses a freedom, a coolness, but rages fire amongst her children.

---

[10] *Michicago Schedule of Events*, 2013. The conference is held every spring, and anthropologists and sociologists gather to talk about—well, we tell ourselves stories.

ॐ

All day, my students are sleepy and pale. They are falling snow that melts upon hitting their seats. I go through the lesson plan, introduce them to the Norse gods. I write vital information on the board. I tell them about common error and how the further back you go, the greater the error. For example, Atlas held celestial spheres, the heavens, so to speak. He did not simply hold up the earth. Then, I say, Write me a five-hundred-word essay about how you could be a Norse god. One student asks if this is a personality test. Other students look around at each other, confused.

My brightest student, a pudgy brunette who always wears a skirt with tights, raises her hand: "Do you mean 'What Norse god would we be, if we could be a Norse God?' I don't understand what you mean by *how* we could be one." I smile and tell them all to just do their best.

After they finish and pass their essays to the front, I tell them the simplest thing that I can.

"The gods are dead. And my own father is dead. You will hear many stories about this, but the only true one is mine. When you lose your father, you are accosted by a million old stories, and a million more are created. It is necessary to build one that you can rely on. I have thought often how I should begin."

They stare at me.

"He was the god of innocence and purity, but he was neither innocent nor pure. My father never knew himself. I am his only son: Forseti, god of justice."

Then, I dismiss class. A few remain seated, to make sure I don't kill myself with chalk.

At the end of the day, I am reminded by Dr. Wilkins, our department chair, that I'm up for review in the fall, and that if I don't have a publication, it won't be pretty. His office reeks of dusty books and cologne. He says, You understand, and extends his hands to me, as if offering up a gift or a sacrifice. I understand.

At the end of the day, I stand outside on the walkway, smoking. I'm not afraid. I am cold and feeling lonely, like that empty fountain in front of the library. When I was younger, my brother always showed me how to do things. He always said, "Joseph, just watch." "Joseph, just listen." And I just faded out, away. He said, "Joseph, you're so weird."

At the end of the day, I disappear. I leave my teaching assistant, an unnaturally tanned (orange) girl, to take care of my class. She's sympathetic and greedy enough to do so and not report me. Claire and my students e-mail me and call me at home, but I don't respond.

"My father never knew himself, perhaps because he did not grow up with mirrors. Instead, the hall of his childhood, Valaskialf, was weighed down by silver."

No, but that isn't quite right.

In mid-April, my brother calls me. He reminds me that he will be here soon. He says that we should go visit Mother's grave in Skokie.

When our father died, my parents had been divorced for several years. V. and I felt no real attachment to him. A sad longing for childhood, but nothing more. When our mother died recently, we split. Our anger about her death was directed at each other, or else we just had never been bound by more than her.

This will be the first time in years that I've seen him, though I have read his articles and books: "The Louisiana bayou presents us with a female figure caught in the liminal space of both the disappearing American South and that of French immigrant culture."[11]

---

[11] *Anthropology of the Americas*, vol. 26, a reputable journal for those who care about such things.

V. says, "No one else visits her, you know."

I tell him that I pay a florist to put flowers on her grave every Saturday. He says that it's not the same. He says we should also visit our father's grave, which is not right next to our mother's but in the same cemetery. A family reunion. V. says, "They never really did anything wrong by us, you know. I'm not sure why you're so angry with them."

I say, "I'm not angry. There just isn't a point. They're dead and gone."

He goes on about the grieving process and showing respect for the dead, showing the smallest bit of respect.

I will try again.

"When a child-god, my father Balder had two younger brothers, Höd and Hermod, to play with under Valaskialf's dome of silver. Yet, Balder and Hermod avoided Höd who had been blind since birth. Höd frightened them with his needs. Balder and Hermod were not so different from their parents in fearing Höd. It was rare, after all, for a god to be blind. And my father was the favorite child. Later, though, when it was time, my father brought his brother to live with us at Breidablik. When I myself was a child-god, I craved my uncle's presence. His eyes glowed from the ease of not seeing the upside-down world. His eyes glowed from the absence of emotion. I was the only one who would look deeply into his eyes. And for not being looked into much—longingly, questioningly—his eyes, too, glowed.

My uncle and I would walk the mirrored halls of Breidablik. From both sides, we were flanked by armies of blind men and children. My memory of Höd is just this: safe like infinity, light upon light."

At the airport, my brother wears a fedora. On the drive home, he requests Chicago-style pizza.

A Wednesday in the white city, and the most popular pizza place is deserted. We are served quickly and our food steams our faces. Then, outside, the wind washes it all away, the heat and the food and the heat of the food.

At my apartment, I remind my brother to wash his pizza hands before touching the Eddaic apocrypha. He reminds me that he's been handling manuscripts much longer than I have. I yell at him, and he puts his hands up—*I surrender*—and goes out onto my small balcony to smoke. I stay inside and close up the manuscript in its leather binding and pet the manuscript, as if to soothe it, as if to say, *No one will part us.* Outside, the low clouds descend on my brother and my city. The monochromatic world breathes life into the old stories—and feuds. We're up all night, me explaining to him my find, my project, and him saying in several different ways that this manuscript is a hoax.

The next day at the University, we run into Claire. She says, "V., I loved your article in *Ethnology.*" He blushes a little—but it's all deception. If you watch, his head is raised and he looks directly at her with a half smile. My brother is confident. My brother swaggers while standing still.

Claire twists her hair and says, "Well, how about we all do dinner?"

"One night in his tenth year, my father Balder had a dream. He rose through the dome of silver and the Wind carried him east of the sun and west of the moon to a mortal castle. In the main room, Balder found his mother dead, hanging from a tree—by her feet. A spiny plant covered all of her body except for her eyes. They remained open. Bugs and worms slithered back and forth between her body and the plant, which were almost one.

A young boy always approaches his mother when beckoned. And though Balder was not beckoned, he gravitated to his mother's side. His fingers danced through the thick vines and branches. He caressed his mother's hair. The hair felt different, just an odd roughness. He pulled a strand and studied it. Ridges and bumps, a dark brown like mud. Her hair was like the vines around her, was the vines. In his hand, the vines and branches turned to sky, to white. As she died, her hair became the white and filament. Her hair died in his hands. You can only see white against dark, and he saw the white against the darkness of the tree.

And then his mother's eyes moved to focus on something behind him. She was alive! Balder turned as his mother struggled in her vine-cage. But he saw no one.

'What is it, Mother?' he asked.

She looked at him, and he knew she was dead and undead and also saw death, that death should come to him when his mother's hair became gray and like thread. A dream and dream-truth."

> To that god his slumber
> Was most afflicting;
> His auspicious dreams
> Seemed departed.[12]

We're seated at one of the best tables, near the large oriel. Claire has worn a short purple dress, and she has her hair up in a high bun. V. has on gray slacks and a tie. I've worn jeans, a t-shirt, and a corduroy jacket. I brought my satchel, in it the Eddaic apocrypha and all of my translation. I'm hesitant to put my translation into the computer or to leave it at home. Until today, I haven't left home for more than an hour. In the windy city, you can get everything delivered—by the wind. Ha.

"The city is nicer at night," Claire says. "The black and the contrast of the lights. Everything is so indistinguishable in the daytime."

"I concur," V. says, but he smiles as if to work his own pompous diction.

---

[12] *Lay of Vegtam*, Thorpe's translation. Yes, he was obsessed, but he is remembered.

"I don't care for it, ever," I say. "If I could spend the rest of my life in Hawaii, I couldn't leave soon enough."

Claire laughs and proposes that we ask the waiter for tropical drinks. I tell her they probably cannot serve those here. Too much alcohol. They have to keep us under control.

After appetizers, I rise to go the bathroom. V. asks me why I'm taking my bag. He tells me to leave my bag. I hesitate, but Claire says, "Yes, leave it."

I know what will happen, like a story I've heard a million times, but Claire looks so pretty tonight.

When I return, they have the original manuscript on the table. They know better, but they're drunk and my brother is trying to ruin me. I cannot help but be furious, as I know this is my brother's doing, my own undoing. Claire would never. As I lean over to snatch it away, Claire knocks over her wine onto the manuscript. She knows better, but she's drunk. We all dab at the manuscript with napkins for a little while. Then, I realize that I'm crying a little bit. I take up the drunken Eddaic apocrypha and my bag. I am outside, and don't recall if V. or Claire said anything to stop me. They're not behind me. I'm alone, blocks away from the restaurant. I don't know where I am, where the nearest train is. I see all the lighted buildings around me, but I don't know which buildings they are. They outshine the stars, but for what?

I'm down on my knees, voicing to the sky, a cry halfway between a child's and a coyote's. Raskolnikov's confession.[13]

Balder never told his mother Frigg the details of his dream. He hoped not to hurt her feelings or frighten her. But he was obligated to tell her that he knew of his own death.

"You must tell no one else," she said, "not even your father."

"I won't," Balder said. "This is a long way in the future yet."

---

[13] *Crime and Punishment* by Fyodor Dostoevsky, whose tombstone reads, "Verily, Verily, I say unto you, Except a corn of wheat fall into the ground and die, it abideth alone: but if it die, it bringeth forth much fruit," from John12:24, which is also the epigraph of his final novel, *The Brothers Karamazov*.

"That will not stop me protecting you."

"You can't protect me."

"I have already protected you," his mother said. "I gave birth to you and saved you from Nothingness. I remain kind to your father and save the universe from Nothingness."

"I'll be a god and a man when the time comes."

She laughed at this. "Only the dead don't need protection." She took a handful of Balder's hair and pulled his face closer. "Do you want to be among the dead? Locked in darkness?"

Michicago begins tomorrow. I have not yet completed my translation or analysis of the Eddaic apocrypha. The wine-soaked pages are still legible, but there are some faded spots. I can extrapolate, though. Perhaps, I already have. When you trace, you follow the lines, but with art, you don't. The spirit and not the letter of translation. You must simply understand.

I stay up all night working. V. comes by around four in the morning. He's drunk. He apologizes again—for everything, he says—and falls asleep on the couch with clothes and shoes on. I don't know what everything is, but I can guess: Claire.

Frigg knew she had to make everything in the universe vow not to harm my father Balder. In one night, she composed a list. The next morning she set out. Frigg first approached Water. She succeeded in securing Water's vow, but Water laughed and claimed her plan was impossible. Frigg moved on. She encountered some difficulty with Birds and fungi, but for the most part, the day went smoothly. Frigg returned home to Valaskialf certain her son would live forever.

When V. wakes up the next morning, I'm in bed. I hear him—the sounds of coffee and eggs. Then, I smell them. I'm exhausted, but it's noon so I get up.

We stand in the kitchen. V. apologizes. He says, "I didn't mean my words or opinions or actions to make you think that I don't respect your research." He pauses to put scrambled eggs on plates for us. "I do," he says, but not looking up at me.

"What happened with you and Claire?"

"What do you mean?" He finally looks up. "No. Nothing."

We sit down to breakfast, but I can barely drink the coffee. Something is bothering me. I believe V. I do. I think I just need to finish the story. I think that so far the story, while more intimate than most, lacks the secrets I seek. Or perhaps I'm in love with Claire. Perhaps, I truly despise my brother. Perhaps, I don't want to present at Michicago or go to my mother's grave. I tell him I'll sleep on it. And the day passes.

You should believe every word I tell you. In the beginning, there was no law, no story. Then, there was a word and the word split into many words. The Old Ones have inspired me. In the end, we must make the laws one, the stories one. This is how one becomes immortal.

My father is Balder. I never hurt my father.

I didn't doubt that my father should live forever. Since before I was born, his impossible death was a joke. His friends would stab him for amusement. But Iron had vowed never to harm Balder. Everyone had great fun pretending. Even I was encouraged to harm my father. But I had secretly vowed never to do so.

After a large dinner one night, my grandmother bowed her head to me and said, "Dear Forseti, if you wish, I will protect you, too." I gazed upon the crowd, my drunken father in the center commanding everyone to try to harm him. I said to my grandmother that I preferred the outer circle.

> In the outer circle,
> We see the ocean of love true
> Is not on closeness based
> We see the pride and assumption
> Too close

Turn away your face.
And learn the outer circle
Where we see, and clearly.[14]

My brother's panel is today. Claire and I attend. She smiles and
again hooks her arm through mine. We sit near the front, and
V. winks at her or at me or at us.

His speech is eloquent, smart. He is the master ethno-linguist.
He receives uproarious applause. He says, "The local bayou
woman is not lost to us. We are lost to her."

When we were children, we put on shows for our mother.
Plays. We did Shakespeare. I was always the bad guy, the betrayer.
I was younger, and I followed V.'s instructions and I thought it
was cool to be the bad guy. Perhaps for other reasons, I was
determined "to prove a villain."[15]

As usual, a celebration for my father's birthday. Candles
illuminated the Breidablik banquet hall, their dim light mirrored
into a painful roar. Light fell from candles and rose from candles
and darted from mirror to mirror, wall to wall, god to god. The
light was gold and the gold was light. Everywhere, we were
bathed in a hundred-fold earthly sunset.

Everywhere, shadows moved to an erratic rhythm, and all
whom the shadows fell upon moved likewise. Mother had her
hair pulled back. As she moved, it jetted behind her, smoke.
Father wore his hair to his shoulders. My own hair then fell past
my shoulders, but my mother insisted that I begin tying it back.

The food was paraded out. Each servant held his piece above
his head. Once all were present in a line, the servants lowered
the food to the table.

Everyone who had been invited attended that night. Almost
in my fourteenth year, I sat at the formal table as well. I sat
beside Uncle Höd, who had taken to humming lately.

---

[14] Eddaic apocrypha, which is its own story of origins.
[15] *Richard III*, 1.1-30. Richard III, who was the last English king to die in battle.

"What're you humming?" I asked.

"I'm humming to remind myself that I'm here," he replied.

Older then, he had trouble keeping his eyes open. In fact, that night, Uncle Höd seemed much older than my father.

I offered Uncle Höd my hand. "Quiet, now," I said. "You are certainly here."

A few seats down from us, Loki. Mother always said Loki was the cause of trouble, but she always said this with a wistful smile. That night, I grinned at Loki from my seat, uttered a greeting.

"Who is it?" Uncle Höd asked.

"Loki, Uncle," I said.

"Oh, he's an interesting one."

V., Claire, and I leave right after his speech. As V. says, we're not here to listen but to be listened to. We head to my favorite sushi place, and it's as if last night never happened. Claire tells stories about her ex-husband and V. about his silly students. I tell stories about our childhood—the plays we put on, the tracing table, the trips to the botanical gardens (the one when V. used all nickels in the vending machine), the day that our mother miscarried what would have been our younger brother and V. said, I've already got a younger brother anyway. My father slapped him.

Claire moves back as if burned by the story. She says goodbye. V. follows her out. When he returns, he says that Claire was upset by the story, that she said she was too close to it. I ask what that means, and V. says that it means what it means. He apologizes and says that he was young and didn't understand. I tell him that I don't care, but he seems sad for having offended Claire.

My mother danced with Loki. He is tall and thin. Loki with his shorter blonde hair still falling into his eyes. He kept touching her hair, running his hand over the length of her ponytail. My father Balder wasn't jealous, though. Like his mother, Frigg, he wasn't the jealous type. But he also knew my mother loved him like his own mother did—to the exclusion of other things. Her dance with Loki merely functioned within her role as hostess tonight. She usually played this role for only the first half of the party.

As she moved away from Loki, I realized she would soon be drunker than my father. Where was he then? He stood atop the table at the far end of the hall. Tonight, his friends, his fellow gods and soldiers, threw arrows at him from all points of the banquet hall.

Loki sat next to Uncle Höd. "What do you think of that?"

"It sounds like much fun," Uncle Höd said.

I closed my eyes and listened to the arrows whizzing. Did they sound like fun? Did their sound change my breathing? Did I smell the air being sliced, feel a breeze, taste speed?

My mother approached then and bade me dance with her. I could not refuse my first dance in the banquet hall. We skirted the table, the chairs, servants, other dancers, candlelight. And soon we were in a corner of the hall right up against the mirrors. I studied my face as we danced. I wondered if my mother's hair was black or a deep brown.

My brother spends the rest of the day on my balcony, blowing white cigarette smoke up into the white sky. I work on my translation until I am stopped by a turn in the story, a turn that I already know: brother against brother.

Later, I watch V.'s sleeping shape. He is small, three inches shorter and at least twenty pounds lighter than I am. He is emaciated from working so hard. He has library skin, computer eyes. He looks anything but immortal on the red suede of my couch, the five-year-old stained red suede. The thirty-two-year-old body of a hero—or a child.

I watched the party in the mirrors. In the mirror world, Loki said, "You should take part."

"I'm not fit," Uncle Höd replied. "I might miss and really harm someone."

"You are fit," Loki said. "Here, take my bow, and I will help you if you wish."

Uncle Höd took aim. Loki guided just a little, for Uncle Höd could hear my father's voice, his laughter, from one hundred feet away. Uncle Höd honed in. A bat or a barn owl.

When his arrow was secure in my father's breast, the crowd cheered as did my father. We were all so proud. Loki grabbed Uncle Höd's hand and pulled him into a hug.

In the mirror world, my father could not remove Uncle Höd's arrow. My father fell to his knees, and the crowd gently took him from the tabletop to lay him down upon the cold floor where he perhaps wished for the silver dome of his childhood, for a more exact fulfillment of prophecy. But he did not rise.

Upon awaking the day before my presentation, V. offers to read my translation. Halfway through, he looks up at me and asks, How much did you pay for the manuscript? When I tell him, he asks to see it. He spends thirty minutes examining it with a magnifying glass, rubbing its folios, recto and verso, between his fingers. He traces the arc of the letters. He sniffs at the parchment.

He says, "Well, you know what I think of its quality. I'm sorry, but I think it's a fake."

"It's not a fake," I say. "The results of carbon dating were inconclusive."

"You don't need some miraculously found ancient document to make your career. It's about doing well with the slow-going. You can't rush it, make it big."

"That's not what I'm after, V. I know that this isn't a manuscript that anyone cares about. It's not the Dead Sea Scrolls, and no one cares about Norse mythology any more. This is for me, for me to understand." He asks what I want to understand, and I say, "Justice, I guess."

He rubs his eyes. "Where did you get the money?"

I tell him that I sold our mother's house in Skokie. He says, "How could you?" and that, "You had no right" and that we were co-owners so how could I—"Yes, I know," I say. "I forged your signature."

V. storms out, and there is a rainstorm coming. I think I hear him on the street below, five stories down, yelling. You can hear him yelling all the way up here.

A ritual. Song, repetition. Father's largest ship. My mother jumped upon his incinerating body. Her bones burned like dry wood, his like a fine sword. Lightning across the water and soon a firefly on the horizon leading the way to another land. The poisonous mistletoe burned, too, but upon a stone altar on land and quickly, too.

V. is gone. He's been gone all afternoon and into night. I present my paper tomorrow. I haven't finished yet. But I can't concentrate with my brother out there, mad at me. He wanders down the gray streets, huddled against the wind, his anger keeping him warm, his anger not washing away.

Grandmother Frigg sent a messenger to ask Hell to release my father. Hell put forth one condition: every object and person, alive or dead, had to shed a tear for Balder. Frigg agreed. She was absent for weeks fulfilling the condition.

Breidablik suffered during these days. I wish I could say mirrors cracked and lay in pieces upon the marble hallways. That our footprints were bloody.

Uncle Höd hid in a dark room, for he saw, though blind, the look in my grandfather's eyes. And he knew well and for the first time that he had never been Odin's favorite, that he had been, in fact, the undesired son his whole life.

I approached Uncle Höd every hour. "Can I help you, Uncle?" I asked. But he did not answer until the twelfth hour after my father's funeral.

"Did your father love you?" he asked.

"My father loved arrows and swords," I said.

"Did your father love me?" he asked.

"My father loved arrows and swords," I said.

"He was my brother, and I loved him." Uncle Höd rose from his chair and pulled back one of the shades. "I can feel the light some days. It was like that with Balder when we were growing up. I could feel him sometimes."

"I was proud of you," I said, "for what you thought you were doing last night. It was Loki who *knew*."

"The deeds of the hands are all that gods can see, blind or not."

And so it was true. And so my grandfather Odin fathered a child, Vali, to kill his other child. Vali grew up quickly, and one day after my father's funeral, he arrived at Breidablik.

I stand on the balcony, having almost finished the translation, knowing from small signs that the end will reveal the secrets and that it will be worse than I thought. I already know that Höd must die—and at Vali's hand. But what of the boy-Forseti's grief?

The clouds hang tight and still despite the wind. The wind stays close to the ground to haunt us. Chicago is the white city because we made it so in 1893. The World's Fair, the Court of Honor. Our city is nicknamed for a city built within it. We impressed the world with our white city. White stucco that glowed. The Administration Building, the Agricultural Building, the Manufactures and Liberal Arts Building, the Mines and Mining Building, the Electricity Building, the Machinery Building, and the Woman's Building. I wasn't there, but I've seen the pictures. A real city—as viewed from within or from out on the lake. It was written that "beneath the stars the lake lay dark and somber, but on its shores gleamed and glowed in golden radiance the ivory city, beautiful as a poet's dream, silent as a city of the dead."[16]

[16] William Stead, quoted in *Devil in the White City: Murder Magic and Madness at the Fair that Changed America* by Erik Larson. Everything is in my city.

༝

Uncle Höd was killed in a dark room.

I watched as my new uncle Vali approached. Uncle Höd kneeled and turned his head upward, as if for food. Then, the sound, of flesh pulled apart. Then, the silence. Then, my new uncle, Vali, approached me with his bloody sword.

"Where is Loki?" I asked.

"Forseti, I'm not here for Loki," he said.

"Why have you not punished him, too?"

Vali shrugged and smiled and walked away.

Inside the dark room, Uncle Höd's eyes still glowed in death. I burned him alone. His body smelled of sweet wine.

When we were children, V. was always in charge, the typical older brother. My father died when I was nine, V. fourteen. V. said that he would take care of me. I suppose he did. He showed me how to do well in school. He showed me how to be strong for our mother. He showed me how to speak and act dispassionately so that no one had to take care of me.

Grandmother Frigg returned from her journey in tears. One giantess, Thokk, had refused to cry for Father. Grandmother told me Thokk was an arrogant giantess. I told her I would take care of it, and though Grandmother beseeched me not to, I went out to find Thokk.

When I found Thokk, I commanded her to shed one tear for my father.

"Forseti, I will not cry for a man I don't love," Thokk said.

"Everyone loves Balder," I said. "He is Odin's son."

"I don't love Odin either," she said, and laughed.

Thokk doubled over in laughter, and as she raised her head and peered at me through her long, blonde hair, I knew it was Loki. I grabbed him by the hair and pulled him behind me.

The Aesir let me decide his punishment:

Let his son be killed. His son's intestines will bind Loki to a spot in a dark cave. Above him, a snake's venom will fall, drop by drop, pronouncing each moment of his punishment. His wife should always be by his side, both of them condemned to wait for release. She will not choose to let him die if you give her a bowl for the venom, but eventually the bowl will fill. As she empties it, the venom will fall into Loki's mouth. Loki will die slowly in the dark. He will know the sting of losing a son, each drop of poison causing him to struggle against the bond of his own son's entrails. His wife will, too, and she will also know what it is to raise her mouth up to Hell upon Loki's demise.

This is the punishment for trickery: poetry. In other stories, Loki's punishment was for a different crime and was delivered by the gods, collectively. This changes everything. Such a punishment placed at the feet of the God of Justice!

I break out the scotch and drink to the irony. No, not the irony. To the uncontrollable anger of the God of Justice who is known to sit upon his throne in Glitnir. The eloquent lawgiver:

> Forsete, Balder's high-born son,
> Hath heard mine oath;
> Strike dead, Forset', if e'er I'm won
> To break my troth.[17]

I'm left alone with a foggy mind and the rest of the story, Forseti's final days.

The Old Ones are half-gods, truth be told. Their job is to actually go out into the mortal world. In Asgard, they do not feel old. Once in the world, they feel skin moving, slipping away from bone. Lips like raisins. Fingers clutched and stubborn.

For the world of men, for a code of laws, the Old Ones

---

[17] *Viking Tales of the North* by R.B. Anderson. What is a lie?

travel. In a matter of weeks, they must accumulate a vast collection of laws, and this collection will be the code of justice and will end conflict. I am to oversee their safe passage.

I watch as the Old Ones trek the spring land pockmarked with white patches of holdover snow that cannot tell of winter's darkness or mischief. I watch as the Old Ones gather the mortal laws in order to make one system. Each Old One furiously writes as a townsman speaks with his face to the sun, smiling and ready to accommodate anything in the light. The grass drowns in winter's water. Water that runs down, drop by drop, until the grass drowns. The grass, too, is white, so you must watch carefully to see. Watch.

I awaken from deep sleep. My brother is shaking me. He says that I must wake up. It's time. Time for what? I ask. He says, Your panel. Your presentation, it's in one hour. We have to go.

We rush on the sidewalks, slipping a bit with speed. In the Hilton, my brother double checks the schedule to make sure we have the right room. Then, we are on the glass elevator, moving up through the world of Michicago, scurrying geniuses everywhere below us.

"I wish you'd asked me," V. says.

"I didn't think you cared," I said.

He stares at me. "Have you been to her grave? Even once?" He pulls at his jacket. "Are you ready?"

"I'm ready."

The Old One Bruadar speaks with an ancient townsman named Egill, who wears a cloak and keeps his head to the ground. Egill refuses to share his town's laws. They argue. The Old One Bruadar remains calm and repeats his question, but the old man pokes holes in the earth with his walking stick each time he says no. Egill talks on for a while, then walks away, the earth sucking at his feet.

"Our winters are longer here," Egill says, over his shoulder.

Bruadar says, "No law can fix that. The earth will freeze when it wishes."

I'm not ready. I thought I wanted to tell the story. As I sit at the table, the white table cloth and the water and the sounds of concerned scholars murmuring—I don't know what story it is that I have to tell. A variation on a truth. A spin on a lie. My brother sits in the front row, and Claire sits next to me at the table. The table from which we pronounce unto the masses. What secret? What the hammer and what the chain?[18]

The moderator announces us. She is some eager student of Claire's. She says that I am the eccentric Norse mythologist.

Upon my turn, I stand up and tell them about how Atlas and Forseti are dichotomies. Atlas was punished for this trickery, left to hold up the burden. Forseti embodied justice. Yet, I tell them, both men weighed and endured a great burden. Does not the judge betray the punished as Atlas was the betrayer by virtue of his brother's actions? Forseti had no brothers, yes, but he knew of brothers. He watched them, their betrayals. I tell them that at the end, at Ragnarok, Forseti was nowhere in the fight. He had released his burden into the world. What became of Atlas? I tell them that I don't know. Hercules may or may not have saved him. It depends on which version you believe. I tell them about myriad texts and documents, the variations, how the variations are greater when it comes to the ever-so-popular Greek mythology. I tell them that there are even variations with Norse mythology, just between the poetic and prose eddas. I tell them that there are more manuscripts out there, some that people don't want us to find. The gods and mythology have become part of mainstream morality, meaning Western morality, and the second we move away from story-as-lesson, the system will collapse. We must compare gods. We must find one story in another, even if that "other" story doesn't exist.

---

[18] "The Tyger" by William Blake. I will paint a pretty picture to go with my story.

Then, after we've all presented, the questions. Most are for Claire. Pirates are exciting!

There's only one question for me: "How are myths moralistic?"

The Old Ones pile into a too-small boat. A pair of sailors mans the vessel which will take the Old Ones to a private island where they can review the laws. Eventually, they will decide on a single set of laws, one system, for all. From Asgard, we will attempt to maintain these laws. The sea today waltzes its happiness.

But then. The boat takes on water, and the Old Ones shake— fear and cold—but hold their documents high above their heads. Only one document is lost, and its ink melts across the page before hiding in dark water. The Old Ones begin a prayer to me.

Forseti, the Old Ones cry, is there any end to the water of earth and sky? Is there any name for the storm so that we may curse it? Is there any law that the storm may be punished? Lead us out of this storm that we may finish our work.

They repeat their prayer quickly and even manage a uniform rhythm. I can hear them clearly above the storm. I am impressed.

But this is not my place, the sea. I am not the god one calls upon for maritime rescue. I must remember they are doing my work, though. Before punishments can be determined, one must formulate the law. I consider Uncle Höd in the midst of thunder and sea spray. Is it true that we are punished for the deeds of the hands? You will have to tell me some day.

After my presentation, Claire shakes my hand and tells me that I did wonderfully, that I presented them with a true conundrum. She's that kind of woman. V. approaches us and simply gives me a head nod. Then, some audience members approach her, as if she's famous. I suppose she will be soon.

I walk away, and V. follows me. We walk in silence. I tell him that I'm sorry. And then we are going down in the glass elevator, walking on gray sidewalks, and snow is melting on our hair—

V.'s hair already, as they say, salt and pepper. And then we are on a sidewalk atop an embankment, looking out over Lake Michigan. The dreary lake, infested with bacteria. The dreary city, snowing in April. Chicago is on the tip of my nose, laughing as a young man laughs.[19]

And then we are in my car, driving up I-94 to Skokie.

When we were children, V. was my hero. He was the older brother—bigger and smarter. He could have been a football player as easily as a genius.

When our father died, V. and I were outside with him, playing football—or throwing it around. Our father stood with the football in his hand. We waited breathlessly, to see where he would throw it, trying to see before he actually threw, studying his eyes and his forearms. The wind blew his hair into his eyes, and then he was on the ground. His eyes like middle-of-the-night and his throat gurgling. I took the football, and V. tried CPR. He told me to call for help. I stood there. V. told me again to call for help.

An aneurysm. An explosion of blood, *of life*, and our father was dead.

When our mother died, it happened slowly. She had a series of strokes.

What happened to their minds? Us, sprung forth like Athena.

The story of my father's death reveals nothing about him. I have told you my father was the god of innocence and purity, but he was neither innocent nor pure himself. At night, I have dreams in which he comes to me wrapped in mistletoe. But he says nothing. I fear he's passed on his emptiness to me. I am the god of justice, but I am not just. I favor the darkness of the cave.

Should I begin again?

---

[19] "Chicago" by Carl Sandburg, a poet who was also a reporter. Which was his truth?

୬ৎৎ

At my mother's house, our old house, on a cold day, a day too cold for May anywhere except Chicago. V. insisted we drive by, just to see. A mother and son are in the front yard. We stop. The wind is brisk for May, but the boy doesn't wear a coat. His mother looks angry, which is why I'm worried when V. approaches her. He explains how we used to live here and just want to see the place again, one last time. He shows her his license, asks if she recognizes our last name or remembers buying the house from us. He says something to her quietly, and her eyes tear up. She welcomes us. She says, Go on in.

Inside, she guides us through newly painted rooms. The walls I used to know are now colors they were not. Carpet stripped away for shiny hardwood.

In the backyard, V. kneels and cries. I've never seen him cry. I wonder if he cries because he couldn't save our father or if he cries for the turning point, the point after which our mother was all alone—save for us, the boys, the children who could only watch. V. clutches at the dead grass. The new owner clutches her son to her, frightened by V.'s grief.

We go back to the car after a few minutes. I tell V. that I don't want to go to the cemetery, that I will stay here, wait on a bench until he comes back for me. He tries to work his eloquence and his swagger, but I'm not swayed. I won't even go near the car. He yells something at me, about how heartless I am, and then leaves.

I stand outside my mother's house, amongst the cherry trees. The new owner peeks nervously out of her windows, wondering why I'm still here.

I cross the street. I stand apart from her and her son and think of Claire. Cherry trees overtake this neighborhood. They are everywhere. While watching my mother's old house, I grab a twig from a cherry tree. I wonder why I agreed to come, how my brother can be strong and then crumble, who this new owner is and if she has any respect for history. I wonder at my own anger. I wonder where the blind man is when you need him.

୬৶

My father died when I was young.

The most difficult stories to tell must be told again and again, to defeat the mirrors.

I place the Old Ones on a small island just offshore of their original destination. Here the land is a pure green, and the sun bears down most of the year. The Old Ones can finish their task in comfort. As they offer thanks, I pray that I may become a different god.

The translation is finished. My brother is gone. He never came back to pick me up, so I called a taxi. I left his stuff outside in the hallway. In the middle of the night, in the middle of a dream, I think I heard him come to get his luggage. I heard him sigh and lug it all away. I'm left with a strange sense of happiness, a forgetting and a forgotten emotion.

I begin to move away from the story. I return to campus. I walk with a sprightly gait. I tell Claire thank you, profusely, for the opportunity to present on her panel. I promise Dr. Wilkins that I will be ready for review in the fall. I check my e-mail, and I read my students' essays, back from the beginning, back from when I asked them to tell me about how they could be gods. My pudgy brunette writes, "I would blind myself so that I would know what comes next and so that I couldn't see what is happening right now." I try to remember what she looks like. Throbbing between two lives.[20] The words become fog and fog boat siren. I try to remember what my brother did to me, exactly, and where he has gone. Where is my father, and where is my mother? Where are Claire and Haskell Hall? Where are the winter and the snow? What has the heat melted away? What am I doing here, up in the sky, above the city by the lake? What are the names for things, for people, the rules, and what do they matter? Am I my brother's keeper? What is the color of blood or poison or love? What is the color of white?

---

[20] "The Waste Land" by T.S. Eliot, a poem of the end.

Foundling

S he was born in curtains, curtains with a pattern of flowers and curtains that felt like flowers but smelled clean, like midnight from her second-story bedroom window. These curtains, they aren't thin like paper. That's what a smarter girl would say. These curtains, they are thin like flower petals. Try looking through a flower petal. And this is how she first sees her mother, on a leather recliner that creaks and moans. This is her mother, silent.

Her mother is gone now, left them for some other city far away. Noise fills the house because of her father, a tall man with hair that crackles when he runs his hands through it. He cries and yells at the ceiling. He throws food into the sink and then lets the garbage disposal run too long. Empty metal clanging.

Finally, one day, he stops the noise and brings the young girl out from the curtains. "What are you doing there?" he asks. And when she doesn't answer: "Well, I've got you now. We're going to be okay." A smarter girl would not have believed him.

The envelope says *overdue*, like library books. She got her own library card a month ago. She reads stories about old things, like swords and magic and large trees. These make her feel safe. She reads and the house is quiet but the words are loud in her head where the dragon and dragon-rider bond and kill danger. Where the magician saves the princess. Where a stone is not a stone, a flower not a flower.

The envelope is new, thin like paper. The girl opens it because she knows how to take care of overdue library books. Inside, a large bill for what are called *utilities*. Water, gas, electricity. Just add wind, she thought, and you'd have all of the elementals. She's read about elementals. Without wind, or any one, the elementals wobble out of balance.

For a while, her mother's things disappeared. They return now as the girl turns thirteen. An eight-by-ten picture of her mother sits on the scratched dining room table, next to a vase of tall flowers. A feminine jacket, practical but almost as soft as velvet, hangs on a brass hook next to the front door. If the light shines through the side window just right, the girl can see the holes her mother darned. Don't let anything in, her mother used to say in the winter months. Her mother's voice on the answering machine, asking you to call back. Come back. Backwards motion picks up speed. Her thirteenth birthday races toward her from long-ago, and she braces herself with all she can find.

Something has changed. Her father spends hours in the bathroom. Tonight, when she asks, he says he is praying.

He's got her trapped. Tonight, she's supposed to present her AP Biology project at an open house. *The Destruction of Hydrogen Peroxide by Various Catalases at Varying pH Levels.*

Tonight, she knocks and he doesn't answer, so she picks the lock with a paperclip, and there he is, silent. He clings to himself and sighs in response to her questions. The pungency of rubbing alcohol. He has written "see her die again" in permanent marker and then tried to scrub it out. She can't leave. A piece of her father's crackly hair has fallen onto the counter. The girl places it on her thumb, blows and makes a wish. A smarter girl would have cried.

She's on her first date, wearing a thin dress. Here is a boy with light hair and full-round eyes. He asks serious questions. They both stare at their plates as she tells him about her mother leaving. The whole time, the boy holds her hand and puts light pressure on the veins, one at a time. Does this make her blood stop? He doesn't ask questions about her father, and she decides she will fall in love with this boy. A smarter girl would have.

On the way to the car, he picks her a pink azalea. She can feel his hand through her dress. And she wonders if this is how it begins. If this is how you forget to protect yourself from sadness, how you forget to leave your child with a kind shepherd. But then, the boy kisses her, and she is back in that garden of clean flowers, watching.

Theory of Everything

Erie reflections easily overtake the boring classroom. Clouds race by outside, and this volatile dimness creates our alternative-dimension selves on the windows. Our doubles waver as in funhouse mirrors, fading in and out like ghosts relative to the darkness flung upon the day. Sometimes you get a peaceful flux of light and dark, waves of each, but not today. This afternoon, the world is outright sick.

Mrs. Jordan rickshaws up and down the aisles with her homework tray, saying, "Drop it in, now." After all the show, she places our papers on her desk. I can see that she's gauging the stack, determining the number of us who are conscientious and those who need to be spoken to about how life starts now, in sixth grade, so do the work.

She's pretty apocalyptic, Mrs. Jordan.

Our alternative-dimension selves laugh and frolic in shadows of our world while we suffer through sixth grade, its biomes and *Flowers for Algernon*.

Parallel universes are scientific fact, quantum physics. The unpredictability of particle movement ends up in one observable movement, which some physicists call collapse. In the 1950s, this guy Hugh Everett, still a student, thought long and hard on this. Maybe he didn't like the word collapse. He eventually realized that just because we can't see all of the possible movements doesn't mean they don't all take place. Connect this theory to reality ideas about reality and you've *got* to have other realities, none of which need to prove they exist. Belief is another matter. Would you believe that in parallel universes stars shine green?

No one believed Everett. This is what drove him away from theoretical physics and into working for the Department of Defense. Everett became a multi-millionaire. He was also an alcoholic and a chain-smoker who died of a heart attack at fifty-one. These are the scientists they don't tell you about in school, but the books are always there.

At home, Mother is the opposite of Mrs. Jordan, asking nothing of me and sucking the light of day, even its refractive glory. While I eat, she watches the Discovery channel on our small kitchen television. Something about dolphins mysteriously dying.

The front door shuts. We both jump, but Mom's slow to react. I stand quickly.

But it's just my father, who my mother sizes up faster than I do. She is holding his face before he begins to speak. His own mother has broken her hip.

Is it possible that dolphins commit suicide like whales? There is sadness in the sea. Maybe portals to parallel universes open up and the dolphins just can't take what they see on the other side, a world of desert sand. Water stabilizes portals and destabilizes the mind. Here we are, flying above the Atlantic on our way to see Grandma. We're offered snacks. Dad considers his mother. He tells my own mother that he used to love Grandma Bowlin, that they did science projects together, watched *Star Trek: The Next Generation* in the very beginning of its run.

He rubs his beard. "We never had an argument," he says. "I should have kept in touch."

"Silence isn't always bad," my mother says.

I sense this is all a show. Rather than prepare me for the truth, my parents distract me, even make me feel sympathy for my father so I won't be angry when I finally discover why I've never met my grandmother.

Grandma Bowlin probably hates my mother. Or maybe she went insane a long way back. Or maybe she was a brilliant scientist and her genius skipped a generation to land on me, who my parents refuse to enroll in private school. She will adopt me and finance my IQ right into the 300s. Dad always says I'm so much like his mother, that I have a lot of Bowlin genes in me, which never made sense because he was the only Bowlin I knew.

"How're you holding up, Addison?" my dad asks.

"Okay," I say, studying the in-flight magazine, a mind-numbing article about spas.

My parents switch seats.

"Addison," my father whispers, "I know this will be the first time you've seen your grandmother. I think you must have questions about why." He places his hand on the top of my head, a gesture he quickly retracts.

"I have *theories*."

Dad nods. "Well, I hope you have better luck than I do with proof."

He's just been given tenure, and the university is coming down on him hard for results, a big publication. He says they gave him more money than they should have, not realizing that all botany isn't quick and revolutionary. Long hours at the lab leave him sad. He often comes home and sits in his work clothes too long. He only loosens his tie. And then he stares up at the ceiling, sighing every few minutes.

Mom—well, she isn't as ambitious. She's satisfied as a biology lab technician. She's satisfied staring out the window, appreciating the water for its appearance rather than the mechanics of its motion or the possibility of calculating the force with which we would hit it if we fell. Short, curly brown hair burying her eyeglasses. Balled hand covering her mouth as if she'll need to stifle some sound of joy. I watch my mother the way my father watches me, waiting for a clue.

I fought with them all summer. They had promised for so long that I could go to a private school. Mom claimed it wasn't so different. Dad claimed we didn't have the money. When the school year began, I complained. I did homework weeks in advance and showed it to them to prove that I was right. My mother began to look at me with fear. Then, I stopped. Here's why: Because as much as I despise my school, there's something special about it which I discovered one day after classes ended. At the edge of the playground, the ground slopes down into a forest. I skirt the edge when I walk home.

Three months ago, I saw flickering there.

I approached the trees just as a light rain began to fall. The further in I moved, the less I felt the rain.

But my secret must stay there or it will slip away like Charlie's smarts and I'll get lost in the maze.

Water surrounds us. Light drops stretch into lines—long, poetic dashes. In the darkness, they appear like stars. We enter into hyperspace, and for a moment, that realm is full of stars, is something more than the landing strip, the twenty-first century airport. I can't believe I didn't have to imagine it.

Hyperspace can be considered a parallel universe, but most often it's considered to belong to a single reality. Hyperspace is the messy, unordered part of our universe. The part that sort of overlaps the ordered part. In the disorder, space doesn't exist as it should. Space is condensed. One person's backyard is not the same as another's, though; supermarket, elementary school, and post office don't exist in the same spot. But almost. If you want to move fast, hyperspace is your best bet. Disorder is speed. All you need to enter into speed is energy. Travel becomes like a dream where your will can be satisfied instantly.

Grandma Bowlin is already back at her nursing home. Dad yells at whoever it is that tells him this on the phone. We race to her in our car, on the way to the hospital. To the grandmother who will help me win a Nobel prize. I bet she has eyes like Neil Bohr. And I will be her Heisenberg.

Grandma's room is a black hole. The brightness from the television has been adjusted so that it won't assault her old eyes. I hesitate to go in. Mom stops short, too. Only Dad can enter this territory without fear, call out to his mother: "Mom?" he questions. When we hear her weak reply, my mother and I follow him into the room

Black holes are caused by a strange act of condensing—or collapse. There's that word again. A star falls in on or into itself until its entirety fills a space so small you can't see it. The density causes a gravitational field that makes prisoners of everything, especially light. The only way to prove black holes exist is to observe from a distance, to do the math backwards. Determine where darkness ends and light begins. Radii and rotational speed reveal the center.

Dad cuts on the lamp beside his mother's bed. She looks like a scientist. Frizzy, curly white shoulder-length hair. Glasses. Dissatisfied look in her eyes. She reminds me of Einstein without that goofiness of the big nose and raised eyebrow. Her leg is in a cast, and a leather hoop that hangs from a rectangular metal frame cradles her casted leg.

She says nothing to my father, who sits next to her and studies an aloe plant on the nightstand. He holds up its limp stalks, too yellow. Smells the potted soil.

"Mrs. Bowlin, you remember Addison," my mother says, pushing me forward gently. Her pushes used to be more violent.

Maybe I'm behaving better as I grow older. Or she just doesn't care enough to use the energy.

My hello is a child's whisper, even though I try to sound grown-up. How does she remember me?

Grandma Bowlin stares at me, turning a toothpick in her mouth. "I guess you grew up while I was drunk," she says.

Dad closes his eyes and lets out a sigh.

"I guess I did," I say.

"They think it's a man's disease." She lifts her arm, points the remote at the television with a great effort. The volume goes away.

"Is that how you broke your hip?" I ask. Dad vacates his seat for me. Grandma Bowlin smells sweaty—and a little like berries.

"No, I stopped that years ago. Had to when I came here to this mini-hospital." She removes her toothpick. "Did you notice that the doors slide into the walls? So quiet, too. Like they're from the future."

Do the doors slide into the walls on *Star Trek*? I can't remember, though I watched it in reruns after school for a while. I didn't like it so much, but I guess people used to.

Grandma Bowlin's roommate coughs, and I notice her for the first time. On the other side of the room, barely visible, lies an old woman wearing a huge diaper and a t-shirt. The sheet is bunched at the end of the bed around her ankles.

"She used to be a teacher, like me," Grandma says.

"What did you teach?"

"Math."

"Did you do research, too?"

"Oh, no," she says, squishing her nose at the thought. "I taught high school, and that was enough for me."

My mother pulls the curtain closed between Grandma and her roommate. Then, she says, "We'll be back soon, Addison."

"Probably need some coffee," Grandma Bowlin says. "That's how your parents and people like them get so much done."

I smile and nod a little, even though my parents prefer tea. "So, how long have you been here?"

"Three lovely years," she says. "And I had to get sober just like that. My friend Kingsley, who lives down the hall, was in the same position. He said it was just like Vietnam: nobody gave him a choice." She removes her toothpick, breaks it and tosses it clumsily onto the table beside me. "So, what's the scientific name for aloe?"

A pop quiz. I answer, "Aloe vera." She laughs abruptly. Then, I ask. "Why don't I remember you?"

"Because the last time I saw you, you were two. I stopped answering the phone and then people stopped calling. Your dad didn't know about all this. I had so many friends that he thought people were checking up on me even if he couldn't. But it's amazing how quickly your friends will forget you."

"I don't have many friends."

"It's better that way," she says. "You probably think he's angry at me. I don't think he is. I'm not angry at him."

"He tells me that I'm a true Bowlin," I say.

"I'm sure you are."

"What does that mean?"

"It means you'll live for a very long time."

Cryonics. In theory, you could freeze someone slowly enough to preserve him, body and mind. Ironically, the subject has to die first. Problems arose about crystal formations that could seriously damage cells, but they solved this problem by using a physical process called vitrification, which sounds like something you'd do to win first-place in the science fair. Revival of the subject remains the largest problem. We can freeze people well and that's about it. In movies, a gentle sleep takes hold and aging pauses. *Living* doesn't seem to be the right word for any sort of suspended animation. You can't call that "living a long time." It's more like living in spurts over a long period of time. One century and another are almost the same, seem to exist consecutively for the cryonicist, who travels his own straight line through the disordered messiness of time.

Dad comes back in, and Grandma turns the volume up a bit. She lets her eyelids droop just enough so he won't talk to her.

He sits on the couch against the side wall and motions for me to join him.

"How is she?" he whispers.

"Good, I think."

"We can talk about her if you want to."

"No, it's okay," I say. "But how am I like her? You always say I'm like her."

"She'll tell you," he says. "Just get to know her."

Grandma starts snoring. Either she's fallen for her own deception or she wasn't faking. I want to believe in her coyness, her reluctance. I don't want her to tell me how I am like her.

Mom finds us there. With my hand barely managing to hold up my head, I ask Mom what the hell happened to those dolphins. She tells me not to curse. Television halos her hair, and she reveals the truth: Dolphins kill dolphins for no reason. They use sonar to determine the perfect spot to strike the prey with their bottlenoses. Lungs collapse. Then, dolphin corpses are flung into the air like rubber balls. Celebration.

There is a girl at my school that we all call Girl because that's what she asks to be called. Most people say "Girl" with sarcasm, though. Girl doesn't believe in God. She's always telling us about her search for the elephant that's buried in a field near her subdivision. Look at her digging. Look at us digging.

She tells me the dirt got red because it's soaked with elephant blood. In the distance underneath a large tent, the neighborhood adults watch our progress. They sip cocktails and argue over whether Girl or I will be valedictorian. One woman, a madwoman, races around telling people there is no elephant. *There is no elephant.* No one listens to her. Girl's mother throws wine in the madwoman's face.

I walk toward them, dirt falling from my hair, my clothes. "Look at us digging," I say, and the adults burst into applause.

I wake up in our hotel room. I'm a little embarrassed when I realize I was carried here. But the shame fades as I remember the elephant dream I had. Sometimes I don't understand my dreams, but I know that they were here.

The next day, when Dad tries to sit next to Grandma Bowlin's bed, she tells him to let me sit there.

"Do you like my doorway to the universe?" my grandma asks, moving her broken leg as much as she can to make the metal frame rattle.

"I like the universe."

"Do you, now?" Her eyes come at me slinky-like.

There's something here. It's all relative. Mom and Dad are bored or scared. Me, I'm watching that toothpick in Grandma's mouth.

"I suppose space is still the final frontier," she says, scoffing. "You should find something it pays to explore."

"I don't want to be an explorer," I tell her. "I want to be a researcher."

"Oh, what have you done to him?" she whines low and deep at my father. She turns to her bedstand and shoves a pile of books at me: *Stranger in a Strange Land*, *Rama*, *Foundation and Empire*. "Here, do some research."

These books are most likely better than *Flowers for Algernon*. "I'm not stupid," I say. "I can be a scientist. A physicist."

"No one's doubting that. But you're too young to want to do research."

"Leave him alone," my father says.

"Get out," she says.

"Don't do that."

"He can stay, but you go."

"Why does Dad have to go?" I ask.

"Because he missed his window," she says. "Once upon a time, he was going to be an interesting fellow."

"Addison, we'll leave you alone with her." He comes over to squeeze my shoulder before he goes. "We'll talk later."

Grandma and I are left in the dark room.

"I want to tell you a story," she says.

She tells me about getting married the summer Armstrong walked on the moon, knowing she would never love anyone more than she loved that moment of voyeurism. There was no hope, though, of becoming an astronaut. When my dad was in high school, she went back to school herself, but only so she could get paid more to teach high school. Grandma didn't care about anything, especially not that schoolteacher who died in the *Challenger* explosion. Grandpa later had a heart attack while my dad was in college, but she didn't care about him either. "The problem was," she says, "that I always knew how far away I was from the moon. When you were born"—she points her toothpick at me—"I realized how far away I was from everything. I started drinking."

"Did it work?"

"Just look at me now," she says. "So much reality."

"I don't want to be an astronaut," I tell her.

"Just be happy, Addison," she says. "Don't spend all your time thinking about what you can't have."

But that's not what theories are about. It's what stories are about.

And then I tell Grandma my story. About the alien I met in the forest. A few raindrops sneaked through the foliage and landed on his bald head, but somehow the water didn't roll off. His skin was thirsty. He looked at me with vertical eyes, pale gray. No light in them, but rather light emanated from two points on his neck, from the balls of his three-toed feet.

We talked for a while of everything. He told me that one day I would encounter a woman of such beauty and wisdom that I would balk at what my life had been before. He told me that this woman would unveil me to myself and from then on I would know how it was that *he* came here, now.

Then, the rain broke through the foliage.

"Addison," she says, "are you making fun of me?"

"No, I saw it," I say.

She turns up the television. "Are you sure he didn't just stand there and blink his big eyes?"

"I thought you would understand what all this meant."

"I do," Grandma Bowlin says. "It means you're a sad and lonely little boy who hates school. "

But I'm so much more complicated than that. I'm an endless theory, reaching for outer stretches of the universe. I move to the couch, away from her. "I know more than you do. More than Mom and Dad do."

"Then, calculate how to relax," she says. "And tell me how to arrange my protons just so to be happy."

Aliens are all biology. Those who believe in them have to consider and reconsider evolution, the organic components of life. Still, they also have to consider statistics, probabilities. But only physics lets us approximate where aliens might be, if they exist. If aliens really do exist, we've got to hurry. There's a journey ahead of us.

Major theories based on alien sightings suggest aliens may not all be from other planets, though. Some consider aliens ancient earth creatures in hiding in far reaches of our own planet. Deep below the sea. A more popular hypothesis is that aliens are humans traveling back in time. The premise of these theories is that aliens come to study us, to have assumptions confirmed or denied. Grandma Bowlin, is that really why you came back? To become certain? But I think I would rather she didn't tell me.

She gazes through her metal frame at the television. Light from the hall casts shadows on the room's tile floor. Solid shadows, real shadows that you can keep with you in this dimension. They won't leave you alone. Grandma snores. I try to imagine how I can be happy here with her.

Doors of a Cold Season

"On the threshold of a cold season,
In the mourning ceremony of the mirrors
And the somber community of colorless experiences,
This sunset fertilized from the knowledge of quiet,
How can one to a
Patient,
Heavy,
Helpless,
man going on a journey
Give an order for him to halt?
How can one say to a man he is not alive
He has never ever been alive."
　　　　　—Forough Farrokhzhad, "Let Us Believe
　　　　　in the Beginning of a Cold Season,"
　　　　　[translation by Julie Ellison]

I.

I am a *div* from before Iran, from the beginning of Iran. A young and playful god, or a demon. I have either ruined our lives or made them incredible. We are on a path for grief or glory. I have hopes that are sky-high. The word changes. Which *div* will I be? My mother named me Amir, a king's name, a name meaning king—nothing. My son will have a better name.

ৡৰ্ৎ

Amina says Canada's blankness frightens her. I tell her this is winter and Alberta is history, that a long ago time—but then I cannot think of any history. Our own. I'm running away. *We're* running away from America and American greed. Amina looks at me sometimes, like we're running toward something worse. My research and my ideas and my dreams are my own. No company or government can have them. Americans are brave cowboys who think they have the right to everyone else's dreams. The American dream isn't the only one. My mother said that was the problem with Americans: they only had one dream. A fool and his money are never parted.

Before we left Madison, I received some letters. For two months, someone claiming to know what I had discovered and what I was going to do. The writer threatened to take everything away, so I took everything with me, away to Canada. I took the letters, though I should have burned them. If they exist, there's always the chance that Amina will find them. I don't want her to be scared, but I feel temptation to read them again and again. It's a mystery of who and why. I keep the letters in a folder labeled "metaphysics of inter-dimensional space travel." That should keep Amina away. I can't keep away from these letters, though. I keep opening the folder, reading them, closing the folder. A haunting of America, but now we are in Canada, so why can't I rest and forget?

We drove north. Truth of North—I remember some story about truth and North. The landscape becomes whiter, which I never thought possible. But the sky itself is washed to white. We sleep in North Dakota, and Amina snuggles and her feet are like icicles. I dream of mountains, but we never see the mountains. Amina says the Canadian Rockies are too far away. We laugh about this—*Canadian* Rockies. We eat a big breakfast. Amina craves pancakes and wonders if Canadian maple syrup will taste better in Canada. As we drive, we keep the heat up and the radio off. Amina falls asleep.

We arrive in Edmonton hours later, and she is still asleep with my son inside her. My son of four months. Her belly is a little ball. I wake her, and we check in to our hotel.

I'm glad they speak English here. I don't have talent for French. Amina says if we speak to our unborn son, he will remember and he will be smarter. She says we should hire people to speak to him in foreign tongues. Then, our son can travel our world and be powerful. Aren't English, Persian and Hindi enough? Besides, I speak half-languages: half-English or half-Persian, or I think in English and speak in Persian, or I think in Persian and speak in English. I trip for words. Amina says that if I understood idioms, I would understand America. I don't understand. I communicate clearly, without phrases that turn like ballerinas. I use fit words that I see, actions louder like words.

> December 21, 2049
> Dear Dr. Amir Pirvani,
> I know what you're going to do. I've been watching for a long time, and I have it on good authority that you will ruin lives. Please stop before this happens. If you don't stop, I'll hurt Amina.
> I snuck into your house last night and smelled her panties.
> —Zeroth

Here I am. I became an American cliché when I became a physicist. I was just another Middle Easterner—like Chinese or Indian—to be good at science. I was just another immigrant to make it big, win the American dream. I got a scholarship for a doctoral degree at MIT, and got a job with Transportech before I finished. I made money, and then I met my beautiful Indian princess, Amina. I had everything to offer her, moon and stars. Most people think the moon only affects tidal ebb and flow, but that is like saying the moon only affects most of our world. The moon is movement, watery death and love. And the moon is hopes and dreams, for man, though man cannot live there. We are what we cannot have. Then, stars. Ah, stars are self-sustaining but radiate out into the far reaches of space. You can tell all from a star's light—tell its age and composition. Moon and stars. I had everything to offer her, but it's all about mirrors. A diamond is a mirror. I offered her what I thought was the mirror of her beauty, and I hoped that she would offer to mirror me in return. Or perhaps I offered nothing and believed in nothing.

She loved me. Somehow, she loved in spite of all the things I had, all the presents. I know this now that we have left our lives and possessions.

We wander around Edmonton, walk through Chinatown. The sidewalks are brighter here, the noise lesser. In the early dusk, a Chinese woman's skin looks gray, like the sky, as she dumps hot water on the sidewalk in front of her shop. Her shop is filled with tea, and the tea smells like a tree we had when I was a child. We walk through Chinatown till a food smell stops us. Amina says our son turns over when he smells food he wants. I tell her people turn over in graves, and she stares at me like that bum back home in Madison who asked her where her sari was. Who asked her for a belly dance.

"Amir, I don't need *you* to correct me," she says, and rightly so.

But I don't say I'm sorry.

"Amir?" Kano asks. He is my dear friend, and he is my partner of crime. He comes here later. We both couldn't leave Transportech at the same time.

"Yes, we're here," I whisper into the hotel phone. Amina sleeps in the hotel bed with her belly double full, baby and food. Her long dark hair covers her face, but I know her face. Protected from moonlight.

"Everything is arranged," Kano says. Kano is the planner, the king of plans.

"How?"

"Does it matter?"

"Yes, tell me how. The more I know, the better I can expect and prepare."

Kano sighs, but then he tells me: shipped in parts, lab space reserved, his cousin, a scientist, flying into Edmonton to help. We all meet next week.

"You okay, Amir?" Kano asks. "Everything's set. Don't worry."

"My wife is here. My child in her. If anything goes wrong, they find us, we cannot run."

"She's strong."

"But pregnant," I say.

"We have to do this. Wormholes are revolutionary. Forget the world; we're conquering the universe. This requires risk and sacrifice."

"If anything goes wrong, she has nowhere to go. I need you to understand." I must ask. "Will you take care of her?"

"I will take care of her. I will take care of your son."

I trust my friend, and so I can concentrate now. I ask Kano about the NE emitter, our design, and the construction plans he asked his cousin to help for. His cousin is an expert in electronics. We work through some equations out loud: sine and cosine, and much more. Then, we are done with talking work, and we laugh. Then, I ask Kano about the girls in Japan. Then, he asks about the Badgers. Then, we talk about baby names, and Kano says that Kano is a very nice name for a boy.

Amina says idioms are American. She says every other language speaks clearly. She says it begins with a secret clubhouse and poverty. She says Americans are all little children. I tell her to go back to India, and she laughs. She says, "Don't get your back up, cowboy."

When I was a child, we came to America. We watched the movie, *Coming to America*, and my mother reminded me that I was her king, not just a prince. She said, You'll get the girl but a whole lot more.

My mother died before meeting Amina. My mother would be proud. She always said that after Persians, Indian girls were the most beautiful in the world.

I wish, almost, that my mother could see my wormhole, my Doorway. I remember reading books when I was a child about other worlds, even inside this earth! I loved these books. I also thought these books were too small. Think big, my mother always told me. Not just one life, a million. Not just one other world, the universe.

Oh, Pellucidar, world beneath the world—within a world. I remember Pellucidar. Tarzan, inside the earth. Tarzan got the girl but so much more. I will have so much more. It's hard not to think like a child when my dream is here. Coming true?

Amina is older than me, born in America, and a mathematician. Math isn't like physics. Math is heuristics. Einstein said, "As far as the laws of mathematics refer to reality, they are not certain, and as far as they are certain, they do not refer to reality." But what is the difference between certain and reality? They are the same. The wise man tries to be humble, but math is not humble. Numbers, equations, theorems, corollaries—are not humble. Men seek to be humble only to deceive. The wise man says that reality isn't certain, yet particles act as they should act no matter what we think of this word, *reality*. And the numbers are certain and real, even if we say, "Subjective! Mathematics is subjective!" No, it is us. We worry too much about perception, how the man who was Thomas doubts. We punish him, but why? He is a seeker, and he doesn't believe in "as far." Thomas simply knows there is something else and he must find it. The truth is freed only if we believe in stability.

After a good rest, Amina says she is impressed with the Westin and our Crowne suite. We've never stayed in such nice hotels, she says. She fingers the vase and fake flowers. She places her hand up against the thick shower door. She yanks the down comforter off the bed and prances with her robe of down. I tell her from now on, we will always stay in nice hotels. The men of this world will worship me for the other worlds I offer. I tell Amina we can stay here or travel the universe. There's no Westins out there, I warn her.

The room service knocks on the door. He rolls in a long table, plates with silver on them. Amina and I sit down for a nice meal.

"I tipped her greatly. Because now we can."

Amina corrects me. "*Him.*"

"You are the English teacher?" I challenge, though I shouldn't. She speaks whole languages. Her English is on the spot.

"Maybe the two of us can make each other better. I can make you a better English-speaker."

"I want more than that, Amina," I say. "I want to be the first. The first person sees things as for the truth. The first person, like a child, discovers the parts—and then the whole comes to him, in a brilliant light."

"I know, Tarzan. But I'm not Jane. I just want my husband and my child." Amina eats her lobster with her hands, licks two fingers. She's messy when eating.

"Our dreams can be the same."

"How is your Doorway *my* dream?" she asks. I hand her a napkin, and she slaps it away. "Your dream offers me nothing but solitude."

"Amina, *jan*," I say, "we will have the power. We will say where, anywhere, you pick. And who and when. Forget money. We will have world*s*. Plural. Plural. Plural. That is my grammar."

She eats while we fight on about problems and dreams. And I tell her we should name our child Tarzan. Then, louder. She eats and eats. Food is the way to a woman's anger. We fight and fight. How does she keep eating? Persians don't eat when they're upset.

December 29, 2049
Dear Dr. Amir Pirvani,
You won't stop unless I make you, right?

Remember the Doorway into summer? Summer is cold and gray. The stars won't align for the great bird. Colors fade to white. Your son becomes your father. Your father becomes your son.

Today, I tell you chitty chitty bang bang won't go fast enough, won't take you anywhere. I'll steal your car. You'll be left alone in the snow. I will leave you there. I will make you alone.

Last night, I snuck into your American house and ate the cherry pie. It was still warm and delicious. Forgive me, but I think you can live without. Merry Christmas.

—Zeroth

My Doorway unites two ends, two ending points, black hole and white hole. One takes away and one gives. Together, they represent the universe. When joined, the path is temporary. For years, scholars denied the Einstein-Rosen bridge. But we can hold it open, get our foot in the Doorway, as they say, with a negative energy emitter. The NE emitter floods and causes normal levels to rise enough to open a Doorway. Then, the negative energy bonds with negative energy inside and on the other side. Negative energy attracts without wanting to. As long as negative energy has its effect, the door cannot shut. The two ends are linked, like Siamese twins.

Iran was split like this, too—split like black and white, taking and giving. Ancient gods weren't good or evil, and then Zarathustra. Our split is permanent, or we make it so, and the world only cares about evil now. You can't eliminate evil. My mother said that evil plays games and the fun never stops. She said if you wish to eliminate evil, you must be ready for no games. For a child, games are all, so what my mother taught me was, "If you wish to eliminate evil, you must be ready for everything, yourself, to end." The *div*, the playful god, before neither good nor evil is now evil. But is he? Who says where one door closes it ends?—for that man knew my secret: that *div* is like a darvish, the poor and wise, but also the secret wisdom. He is the one who opens a door. A stable wormhole, a Pirvani Doorway.

Amina has always lived in America longer than I have. She was only six, I ten. Her family is from Madhya Pradesh. When she was younger, her parents made her watch Disney movies to learn English. Her favorite was *Aladdin*.

Amina's English is only better than mine because she tries always. I don't care. Amina's mother told her that I would never make it unless I talked better. I know that story, and I know my story. I'm not underdog. I turn it on and off. Free will. When we go through the Doorway, it will be always on, my power. Only my power, no words.

My friend Kano arrives one day after us. He meets us downstairs. Travels light, so he only has one bag. He is tired but doesn't feel tired. He smiles, big eyes, hugs Amina several times and pretends that he cannot get his arms around her. She hits him on the arms and back. But we are all laughing.

"We are ready?" Kano asks.

"I'm going, too," Amina says. She is jealous. I know her. Her science is not as exciting. She wishes I had no partner. She's jealous of a plan and a friend.

"We're not taking you," Kano says. "Radiation."

Amina stands tall. "Let her come," I say. "She can wear a lead vest, like us."

Amina grows quiet and nods. Her monster with green eyes is ready for battle.

We drive east along 118th till we get to an abandoned building. A warehouse. "A factory," Kano says, "not a warehouse. This factory is small and easier to secure."

The warehouse is tall, like what I think is a castle, and dark, almost black. The warehouse is dirty and the sky clean. The bottom half is bricks and metal doors, some regular doors

and some like garage doors. The top half is windows and the
ceiling is full of vents.

Inside smells of shit and mold. Amina gags and returns
outside. We look around. In a far corner, old machines we don't
know anything about, rusting silently. Kano says printing, and I
say packaging. The rest of the warehouse is mainly blank space,
a layer of dust on the floor like a desert. I don't remember any
deserts: only American snow. My mother says that I grew up in
heat, around sand and mountains. Can mountains be of sand?

Kano goes up some steps and yells down to me, "I found
my office. I'm boss-man!" He comes out and throws a stapler
down at me. He misses.

Up high, there are some platforms, some upper-levels, but
just a few. I feel like the machines they left behind are only the
smaller, useless ones. Whatever machines used to be in here
must have been huge, reached the sky.

"We'll clean it up," Kano says. "Shipments don't arrive for
another two days. I've got a cleaning crew coming tomorrow."

"How will you get the shipments here without suspicion?"

"These aren't normal delivery services. I know people." He
grins to say how business savvy he is, how American. He's
probably more American than I am. I worry. I am scared, and I
am crippled by fear. So un-American. So un-cowboy.

Windows are high up in this factory. Sunlight cuts through all
of the rotten smell. I wonder how often the sun shines here. In
Madison, we didn't get much in winter. Sunlight cuts, but we'll
have to black all the windows. For security. I worry—and Kano
smiles like he's always pleasing the whole world, not just me.

A long time ago, in a fairy tale, Amina and I met. We fell in love,
or I fell in love with her. I think she loved me. After I asked for
marriage and she said yes and then "I do," we had to move to
Madison for my job with Transportech. Amina hated Madison.
She said it was desolate and white. A few months later, though,
she was okay. Okay with weather and football and German food.

One night shortly after we met, in a cold September—already thirty degrees—we went to a piano bar. Amina requested we dance. We were having a wonderful night, the music and warmth of a fire. Then, Amina yelled at the waiter for overcharging us. Amina fights her two sides, strong and fragile. Sometimes, I'm not sure if I should act prince or slave for her. Her brilliance makes it hard for her to be just one kind, and myself, I try to be one. I try to believe she loves me.

We walked home that September night, holding hands, but Amina was crying and would not look at me. We walked by quaint shops, still with paper signs for "open" and "closed." We walked on clean sidewalks and cobblestone streets. The air was cold enough to keep your sinuses open, to keep your mind alert. Amina shivered. She pulled at a dying purple flower on a bush, but the flower wouldn't let go.

I found Kano, the math whiz, a long time ago in a university bar. We drank gin and tonics while he got red of the face. Kano said not to laugh because he couldn't help it. He promised that his face was red but he could drink a lot. We were both students, but Kano was *naqal.* We connived, as Kano says, to make money off exams. His idea. We didn't steal answer keys. We used math and brains to anticipate the questions and answers. Our guesses were usually right, and we rightfully called ourselves tutors, for we were providers, weren't we? Teachers, weren't we?

I got Kano a job at Transportech. After Transportech was contracted by the government, by NASA, Kano and I found another way to be teachers.

My parents were religious, Baha'i. I remember the names of the prophet, his son, his grandson. Baha'u'llah, Abdu'l-baha, and Shoghi Effendi. I remember the Letters of the Living, the Hands of the Cause. Fasting. Seven Valleys.

My mother made me memorize prayers and tablets. I was a reciting machine. When I was seven, we went to the world conference in New York. Up on stage, I recited the Tablet of Ahmad. "O people, if we deny these verses, by what proof have ye believed in God? Produce it, oh assemblage of false ones. Nay, by the One in Whose hand is my soul, they are not, and never shall be able to do this, even should they combine to assist one another."

Everyone said I was cute, "oh-so cute." The boy after me was only a little older, and he performed slam poetry, which I'd never heard before. He slammed his words, and they came at me hard. His arms loose, all over the place, and his body, also loose. But his face. I remember the anger on his face. Mother always said not to be an angry person, for anger is the opposite of love. She said a soul cannot even begin a journey in anger. This slamming boy was angry, and I looked to my mother. She smiled, clapped to the beat. This boy was angry; I was angry. We cannot enter the valleys, pass through to God. My mother smiled.

When I was older, I was no longer *mazhabi*. I didn't decide to. I just grew up. Religion was just another story, and I will remember, yes. I will not return, though.

The equipment arrives in pieces, like Kano said. A laser which he will modify for our purposes, what I call a mini-collider, several laptops, sensors with wires, just wires, and radiation aprons. Kano spends time putting the NE emitter together. I set up the laptops, download our software, and hook up the sensors. Our headquarters is a large card table. The laser and collider when linked will be our NE emitter. A large telescope that cannot see itself but can open the Doorway.

I want to stay with him, but I cannot today. And Kano promises he can do it. Amina and I wander through the city because she feels ill—her stomach churns (butter?)—and thinks walking makes it better. We walk down gray streets, and we look up at tall buildings. The Scotia Place, those twin buildings, which light up against the dark and stormy sky.

She tells me the story of how she was young and supposed to marry a bear. She was with her family in the country, and she kept wandering off. Her father gave her a pair of wooden shoes, just warped tree branches that looked like shoes. Her father told her a bear wanted to marry her and had given the gift of these shoes. She says the shoes felt cold and hard. Amina kept away from the woods because she didn't want to marry a bear. She was scared.

"Why were you scared of the bear?" I ask.

"I was a child," she says. "And I didn't understand his gift of shoes."

Past the city hall, and now at Churchill Square. Amina chooses a bench near the fountain, but the fountain isn't on. There is slushy snow in it. I ask her if I'm the bear.

"I wish that we had a home here," Amina says.

I tell her the warehouse will be our home.

"Your warehouse is a terminal, a thoroughfare, for all of your dreams. It has nothing to do with me."

"Amina, you're a scientist. You understand, don't you?"

"Amir, I'm a scientist, but I'm not smart, like you. I'm not a dreamer, like you."

This is our old problem, our old argument. She thinks I'm smarter than her and that she's better than I am, a better person— not riddled with greed and ambition. I run my hands through my hair, and I hear her sigh, know she's evaluated the gesture.

"I want more than one day out of three," Amina says, "but frankly, it's the best deal I've gotten out of you for years." She stares at the snow. Does she wish it to melt and rise up to form the arcs of fountainous glory? You cannot fight the season. Even I know this. It's the winter, and we must be content.

II.

January 3, 2050
Dear Dr. Amir Pirvani,
You aren't scared of me. I have the vantage of

one looking back on his life—from a deathbed or, worse, prison. So, I'm here and beyond here. Can you understand this? Does such uncertainty frighten you? It should.

Destroy your NE emitter. Yes, I know about it.

—Zeroth

When the very first letter came, I thought it was some sort of prank. I thought, too, maybe it was delivered by Kano. Two days later, I called Kano to make sure he didn't send the letter as a strange joke. He said no. The second time, he said, "Shit. Shit. I may know who sent it, and he's dangerous. If you want to go through with your Doorway, we have to leave now."

"Where should we go?" I asked.

"Where do you want to go?" he asked.

I said Mexico, Switzerland, an island somewhere.

Kano waited, and said, "Canada."

"Canada?"

"Yes," he said, "it's the last place you'd ever go, right? You hate the cold, so why would you go further up into it?"

My friend, Kano, he is a sneaky fox.

We're sleeping in the afternoon. I dream of another world. I'm beneath the earth, and under an always-shining sun. Not Pellucidar, though. This world is another world's subterranean. Air is like water, like womb. I move through and can see the ripples in the air. I open my mouth and taste, and it's like water. Is water like stone, then?

There's a golden bridge over no water but sand. I cross, and look down into sand, moving, too, but not in rhythm with the air. This air in my lungs, and I can feel myself ripple. We're all out of sync. At the end of the bridge, a car-dealership filled with cars and balloons. I'm the two-dimensional clown then, high above. And then even higher, seeing the world in line with many others, all with clowns tethered all the way into space.

Kano calls to say emergency.

"What do you mean?" I ask.

"There was a man sneaking around outside," he replies. "I went out to yell at him, and he pulled a gun on me. He said, 'We found you, and we're not going to let you get away with it.' He shot a hole in one of the windows."

"We need security."

"We can't trust anyone," he says.

"I'll figure it out," I say.

My mother died when I was old enough, not a child, but I was still young. She had breast cancer. After three years, the cancer came back, and the chemo didn't work. She had tumors all over her body, tumors like golf balls the doctors said. I never played golf, but the doctor held up his hand and showed me the size of the ball.

I took care of her as much as I could. Someone paid for a hospice worker to come in the end. Sally. Sally took care of my mother in the end. I sat in the living room, making a list of what should go to whom. I listed the items I desired first. A selfish act of love, but I don't think God watches me to see my crimes.

And this is my first time in a police station. An officer is at the front desk. I talk to him through glass, bullet-proof. "I need to know how to hire someone for a security job."

"We don't do private work."

"Who does?"

"Here," he says, handing me a few business cards.

Then, we three meet with Robert Frusso. He walks with the air of an American movie man, Humphrey Bogart. Frusso is Bogart in dark movies, dark light. He has a long face, keeps a shadow on it, and he wears his suit. Frusso promises protection and discretion, all with a Canadian accent. Amina struggles to understand him, but I can tell she's intrigued by his darkness. Amina asks him what there is to do in Edmonton except eat Chinese food. Frusso laughs, and says, yes, the Chinese food is good, but he recommends the ice fields. He tells Amina to bundle up, though. He says, the ice fields are formed over a "crack," and he laughs, that's called the great divide. He says it's beautiful and white.

We take five of his guards for what seems a cheap price.

When they show up at the warehouse, I am impressed with their size and weapons. We position three outside, and two inside. The two inside are kept at a distance from our work, not that I think they'd know what it is.

"These goons make me feel better!" Kano laughs. "I never thought I'd have my own goons."

"They can save us tomorrow," I say. "Don't call them goons."

Amina laughs. She says, "You guys definitely need goons."

We order some awful pizza. Amina reminds me that pizza, as we know it, is a largely American tradition.

Kano and I shop-talk. Amina interrupts and says she wants to go to the ice fields, but I remind her that they're almost six hours away.

> January 12, 2050
> The end of your life: Snow, falling. Amina won't
> be there.
> —Zeroth

This fourth letter seemed more of a threat to Amina. How would he kill her? Perhaps, he would just kidnap her—and leave me alone. Or kidnap her and blackmail me. Or kill her by cutting my son from her. I've seen the news and the movies.

This is when I made plans to leave. I didn't tell Amina about the letters. I just told her about the people from work, how I suspected they were dishonest. I told her that if I left I was breaking my contract so we had to leave the country.

I was a child when my father died. He worked for an aeronautics company, and in an experiment, he was exposed to a lethal amount of radiation. He wasn't allowed to leave the lab. My mother and I saw him after the accident, and he was thinner. Covered in sweat. He was throwing up into a bucket as we walked in. There was a second bucket, but I didn't know for what.

We spoke goodbyes through a window. My father said, "Don't think danger makes me unhappy. I *am* happy. I served my dream, and I die with *happiness*." My mother took me out in the hall. She yelled that *kosh hali* was for animals, for foxes only when they made the kill—a simple emotion. I wondered what my father had killed.

Inside again, my mother cried. I heard my father yelling. At her? Then, of course, silence. I didn't know what that meant as a child. When older, I imagined them holding palms up to the glass, almost touching. Maybe kissing through the glass.

After the silence, Mother came into the hallway to tell me a story. She waved away all the other men, my father's co-workers and supervisors with lead vests and lead masks. She told me the story of Fereydun, how two of his children murdered the third brother. Then, the third brother's grandson killed the two murdering brothers. Murder and then vengeance. Murder, then vengeance. My mother said vengeance was wrong. Vengeance against whom, I wondered?

Old enough now, I think in that room my mother told my father a secret. I think she told him that she was not in happiness—and he couldn't help us anymore so go ahead and die. I think she told him, "Go ahead and die." But he didn't. For years, my father in my dreams. My dreams of vengeance against a father who left us— but who left a long time before that room, that glassed-in room.

I spend the next day with Kano. We put together his laser, and he pretends to shoot it at me. We work and play together until I know that I must return to the hotel.

At the hotel, with the day fading, Amina reminds me of our agreement. She gets at least one day out of three. I promised. I tell her there's tomorrow, always. She returns to the bedroom, and brings out some math that, at first, even I can't understand.

"You think you know the risks," Amina says. "Forget where you'll end up—this universe or another—or even how you'll get back. If the energy of the Doorway overtakes the regular quantum field, we're looking at a cascade effect. And the math says that this can't be contained once it begins. The math says," and Amina pauses, "that your negative energy, this interaction, is enough to cause a cascade."

"You know math isn't always right. You know it's theory, like everything else. We think we know the rules, but we don't. We cannot construct the proper equations."

She tosses a book onto the bed, then another. Another. Another. Another. And she sighs. "Theory has its place. There." She points at the books. "On the blackboard. In papers. In steps, not in grand gestures. There are too many variables, and if we accept that we don't know the rules, then all we have are variables."

"Amina, you know our research is sound. These theories you speak of—we're beyond that. Our proofs are logical. All theories must be tested."

She begins to pile the books. "You never hear about the theories that turn out to be wrong."

Outside, the day is still a little bright, but I know that the sun is going away, how cold it is. I smell her shampoo, watch her breasts dip as she leans over the bed. *Remember the day you saw her*, I tell myself. *Remember her sitting by the man-made lake beside the white library. White bricks all around, and dark water. The week before you were going to graduate.*

"Amina," I say, "you know I must do this."

She sighs and changes the subject. "Who is this man Kano called you about yesterday?"

"He is against us, but we don't know why." Amina looks at me for more answers, but I have none. "He's a stranger. I don't know why he's here."

"*We're* the strangers," she says, "in a strange land, and now we want to open Doorways to more?"

"Nothing is strange. Everything begins. Don't be afraid."

She sits down with some difficulty. "Do you remember our first meeting?"

"With Kano?"

"No, date. I mean date. You told me how silly your parents were, your mother especially. You said you wouldn't be foolish enough to actually believe in anything. No religion and not science either."

"Yes, and science doesn't ask for belief. I remember." I kneel next to her. "I'm not asking for belief. I don't believe. I'm dreaming, and I think it will lead us somewhere."

"I don't want you to go anywhere."

Amina's parents died last year. Her mother and then her father soon after. With my parents dead, too, we have no one. We have Kano.

"Let's go outside and look at the mountains," I suggest. "They're beauties."

We stand outside. Amina, without shoes and only thick socks and a cotton bathrobe.

"This isn't how I imagined sabbatical," she says.

I hold her close, and her hair smells of flowers about to bloom, so faint, and her head is so warm. I beg her to cook for us tonight, and she says she will if I get her a hot plate and a pan and a knife and if I can find an Indian grocery store. I promise to find an Indian grocery store. I promise to take her out to the Columbia Icefield this weekend.

Then, Amina folds up one of the pages with her math on it, folds the page into a paper airplane. It dives off the balcony toward the snowy ground. I point out to the horizon and say, "Look, can you see those Canadian Rockies?" We cannot. We have only a cityscape, man lighting up the night with his metal and silk ties and dreams. She smiles so big as she watches her plane fall.

I remember the story of Simurgh. The white baby that Simurgh rescued was crying, but great bird Simurgh soothed and taught

him well. The child's white skin became all the colors of the
bird's feathers. The child played, and his time as a child was
longer than others'. He grew up eventually and wanted to return
to men. Simurgh let him go.

The child, now man, found the world of men and a woman
to love. He was white again. My mother said his wife gave birth
to a great hero. I asked "How could he give up such colors?"
My mother said "One way or other, child or man. You cannot
be both."

I remember Madison, the letters. I was so scared. When I left,
they stopped. So no one followed us. But I had a dream last
night, of opening the first. Instead of paper, I peeked in and
saw a video playing on the inside of the envelope.

Green skies, like green eggs and ham, an old story. Then,
something like a bear barreling across the land. My mother always
told me that bears were men that needed love to change them
back to men. Here is the bear, eating some long plant, ripping
at it with his teeth like he would a wild animal. Then, the sky
blinks.

A picture paints words.

Here is Amina cooking. Her hair is pulled back, sweat on her
nose. Stomach too close to the hot plate. I smell lamb and many
spices. She cooks more when she is hungry. She cooks Indian
food when she is hungry, her native food, her first food.

Kano arrives with three bottles of wine, one for each of us,
he says. Kano is the funny one. He goes to hug Amina, again
pretending he cannot reach his arms around her. She tsks him
away. Kano lights a cigarette, and she pushes him onto the
balcony, waving me to go with Kano.

So cold tonight. I smoke, like Kano, but to keep warm. "How
does a cigarette warm you?" I ask.

"Soup warms your belly," he says, "and smoke warms your
lungs."

"Did that stranger come back to our warehouse?"

"Factory, and no," Kano says. "We have a lot to do, but I think we can get it done in two week's time."

"How's the negative energy emitter design?" I ask.

"All good," he replies. "I'm almost done with the construction, and then we need to do the tests."

Amina calls us inside for dinner. She apologizes for only rice, no bread. But her curry is so good, warm and spicy.

"When are you going to cook some Persian food?" Kano jokes.

Then, knock on the door. It's a policeman. He says there's been an incident at our warehouse. A man, the same stranger, threatened our security guards. They got his gun and tied him up before calling the police. Now, this man, this stranger, is at the police station. The officer says the stranger looks emaciated and is asking for me by name. The stranger says he wants Amir Pirvani, the man with the key to the Doorway.

I keep Amina away from us three men as we talk. She's suspicious, but she stays away.

The officer says it's an old man, seems to be no harm. Frusso specifically requests us to come down and look over the old man. We can decide to press charges.

Kano and I go with him.

When she was younger, my mother snuck into her school's office and changed everyone's grades. For fun. When they found out, my mother ran away, and all day long she hid with the rifles. The rifles were in a special shelter beside the house. Four high walls and no doors. You could only get in with a special ladder. This was all to protect the children and keep them away from guns. But my mother climbed into the gun shelter for protection from the adults. She didn't need the special ladder because she was a good climber.

She stayed there all day, with the guns, listening to their worried talk. At night, she snuck into her bed. She was allowed to sleep that night but the next day her feet were whipped with twigs until they bled.

I asked her what I should learn from this story because stories were for learning. She said, "Safety is a tricky thing."

At the police station, the stranger is gone. He's just gone, like a snake, *zah-re-mar*. He is a night thief. The police are not like on American television, but tired and unconcerned. They aren't surprised. They say everyone is overworked and tired. An old man can sneak out, easy, in this police station. One policeman wonders aloud about how an old man could get out of handcuffs. Another says that all it takes is a small metal object.

Kano and I file a complaint. Frusso isn't offended. Instead, he asks us why this man would want to hurt us. We tell him the truth: we don't know.

I know that I have some history with this snake, but I don't know how I know—or what. I remember snake stories. I remember the snake moving sideways to move forward. This old man will keep us watching him, will keep us moving sideways and never forward.

Here is Goda. He is a machine, better than. A machine for love!

Goda is a scout robot. He resembles a small helicopter, uses the principles of such, but he looks more delicate. He looks like a metallic swan. Goda has seventy terabytes of memory. Papier mache of metal. He will travel ahead of us, find brave new worlds and then tell us how brave, how dangerous.

Can two men change the world? This question Amina has asked me several times. I remind her this morning that Kano's cousin helped, that she helps. But Amina says we need more—more resources. I tell her how simple it is. She says she'll come to the warehouse more often. She has experience with computer chips, but I worry about her being in the warehouse with this old man wandering around. He's old, and still, with a gun anyone is young.

♥∽≪

Here is Amina, at the warehouse. Her pregnant belly is almost lost in the dim light. The lead vest weighs her down more. She trudges with what she says is fifty extra pounds.

She sits at Kano's desk in her radiation apron and finishes working on a chip, a regulating chip, for the NE emitter. Kano smiles at her and hammers away at the stand and encasement for the NE emitter. He's expecting backlash and residual radiation, the residual from a potential feedback loop. His encasement must be stable and keep the radiation from escaping. He's also set up what he calls radiation absorbers, RA's, around the NE emitter because he worries in general about radiation. RA's look like those screens they set up behind you when you get your picture done at school.

The NE emitter is our telescope. I suppose it's also a gun. Clearly long and with aiming capacity. On a tripod. A glass gun right now, without its encasing. If I disappear, it will be a gun that smokes.

Kano works hard, and his work is good, with relief and end. My work is mostly in my head. I project and dream. Theoretical physics. Quantum physics. Mostly dreams. I don't need to know what our chances are, the possibilities. Where I could end up. I revel in possibilities.

When we're done today, we have to figure out how I can take the NE emitter with me, or a smaller version, with me, and how to isolate the same Doorway. Or we have to figure out how to keep the Doorway open. Kano says that I should just take the NE emitter with me. I refuse. I say we cannot take the original NE emitter. It's history now.

Kano hypothesizes that the residual wormhole will last a few days, and if I focus an NE beam on the same spot from the other side—then, the original wormhole will open. We keep our gravest concerns from Amina, but she hypothesizes on her own.

Amina tosses in our bed. She speaks in Hindi, very quietly. Before

Canada, Amina slept well, and I've only heard her speak Hindi three times. Her parents wouldn't let her speak Hindi. *Krp-ya.* From her mother, now dead, I know this as *please.*

I whisper her name. She says, *"Krp-ya,"* and I say, "You're welcome." I say, "You don't have to plead with me. You can have anything." I say, "Wake up. You have everything." I say, "Don't have bad dreams. Everything will be okay."

The next morning, we go to the warehouse together. Amina insists on coming. There, we find Kano and his cousin. They're working hard and finishing construction. They say we're ready to test tomorrow.

I pull Kano aside and ask him why his cousin is still here. Kano says we need the help. I don't trust this cousin. He doesn't speak much and always wears a bandana around his head. This is our project, Kano's and mine. We don't need help. We're criminal partners.

Amina and Kano's cousin hover over the internal design, the chip and circuitry. He is impressed with Amina's work. Kano's cousin offers to help more with the problem when we start testing. He can rewrite, if we need him to.

I decide we need some breakfast. I tell Amina to order and go pick it up with one of the guards. We three men need to have a meeting. Amina is suspicious, again, but as usual, she goes.

"Kano," I say, "how soon can we start testing?"

"Tomorrow," he replies. "After some calibration, we can send through a Goda and hope for transmission from the other side. The radiation might make that impossible. The other option is to zap a Goda with the NE emitter, then send it through, hoping its residual will keep the Doorway open or reopen it."

"What technology is the UAV capable of?" asks Kano's cousin.

"Goda." I correct him.

"Ideally," Kano specifies, "video, radio, collecting data on temperature, atmosphere and radiation levels."

"As long as the Doorway is open," I say, "we should get live feed. If the Doorway closes, we have to wait and hope that the sphere returns on its own. Our backup is to miniaturize the NE emitter."

"But we believe that as long as the NE emitter is on," Kano says, smiling, "the Doorway will remain open."

"What about power?" says Kano's cousin.

"Once we're on," Kano says, "the power should be self-perpetuating."

"Well, if you need something else, let me know." Kano's cousin gets up to leave. Kano follows. I'm left alone with the table and the wet cold.

The NE emitter is the size of a larger camera, a camera on a tripod ready to take pictures of other worlds. I hope for one with pink skies and flying birds of many colors. When I return, I'll bring gifts of medicine and beauty. I'll cure our sickness and our unhappiness. I'll be a cowboy, a superhero.

We three eat our breakfast at Amina's insistence. She adds sardines and Canadian maple syrup to her pancakes.

"My cousin had to leave," Kano offers.

"Is he really your cousin?" Amina asks.

I'm stunned that she suspects us of such large lies. And who else would he be? She's obviously jealous. I suspect for valid reasons, she for her own. She wants me for herself, but she cannot have me, as they say.

"He is," Kano says, looking confused. "I speak of him often."

I tell her that those sardines stink, and Amina takes her plate to the single desk in the corner.

"Is she all right?" Kano asks, once she's away.

"I don't know." I chew on some bacon, real Canadian bacon that tastes no more real than in America. "She's jealous."

"We have to stay focused. If she's getting in the way, she needs to stay at the hotel. You have to be separate from her. Work at work. Love at home."

"I know," I say. "How do I tell her that, though? She's pregnant."

Kano sighs and shoves his mouth full of eggs. "We're ready for a test." I don't reply. He continues to eat. "These are cold," he says.

Then, Amina is at the blackboard staring. She picks up chalk.

Amina says, "There's something wrong with these equations. I don't know quantum physics very well, but the balance is off." She puts down the chalk, begins to copy what's on the board into her notebook. "I wish I were smarter for you. I'll work on it tonight."

On the board, symbols that look ancient to me for the first time. Soft lines and hard lines. Lines that separate one side from another. Symbols of a woman's body, a gun, a winding river, a hungry mouth. Hieroglyphs belonging in a tomb. Math is only a means to the end. Amina would make them all, trees for the forest.

Amina left me once. We had been together for almost a year, and I forgot something. A birthday or holiday? I was supposed to get her a gift and take her out for the town. While alone, I thought of my own parents. After my father died, my mother made a book of his life. She told me to read and remember. She never cried. Just once I asked her if she was sad, and she said love doesn't last forever. She said you can't love anyone forever. I miss my mother's stories.

III.

I wake from dreams and feel like morning light. In the early morning light, Kano calls. He says we're ready. I tell him, "I'll be there soon."

Amina isn't in our bed. I find her outside on the balcony. She holds her arms up, like she's flying. She makes a sky angel. She tosses her head back, looks straight up at birds, God.

She turns to me. "I don't want you to go."

"I must go."

"You promised to take me to the Columbia Icefield. When you've done that, you can go."

"Amina, Kano has everything set."

"Oh, Amir," she says. "I just want my time with you."

"You know that I'm not going to go through today, right?"

Amina says, "A test begins everything."

We take a red bus to the Columbia Icefield. Kano isn't with us, and he's mad at me for delaying. But here I am, with my wife on the red bus, heading for what they call the Columbia Icefield, for what they call a "hydrological apex." The glacier feeds three oceans and sits on the Great Divide. As our tour guide continues, I realize that this is perfect. We are in the perfect place. Everything, together—and yet split.

The bus stops and the tour guide gives us permission to walk around, but he tells us not to go too far. "Don't let the snow blind you, now!" he says. How can snow blind? I thought you had to stare into the sun to be blinded. I suppose reflections are powerful, too.

Amina says, "Come on," and we move about at a reasonable speed, for the snow is like carpet. The snow is like carpet and flat, a true floor for us tourists. Amina says the field looks tiled with mosaic but mosaic of one color. We can see the points of meeting—or are they points of separation? How do you tell the difference between beginning and end?

We move to the edges of the group. Amina climbs up a slight incline, and there before us is a bubbling field of ice. The ice is not flat and looks slippery. Here is the furious ice, where the other is peaceful. We stare at this cauldron. Doubled trouble. We watch the mountains dark behind and the clouds bright, racing away.

We return to the group and the peaceful ice. Amina asks, "If I were smarter, would you stay with me?"

I stare at her and say, "You're brilliant, but I have to go on this journey."

Amina squats, then sits. She says, "I expected it to be colder, but the ice isn't that cold." She says she wishes she could give birth here. A baby slipping across the ice into three different oceans. Three different worlds. I like her idea. It is science fiction and poetry together.

IV.

We're finally ready to test the NE emitter, to open a Doorway. We are all here: Amina, Kano, and I.

"Ready, friend?" Kano asks.

I say yes. Amina hugs us both and stands about ten feet behind. Kano starts up the NE emitter, and it makes a sound like a coffee pot brewing. Nothing happens. For two months, we repeat.

Then, on a brilliant May day, there's a black disk, black and brightening the warehouse at the same time. Kano and I look at each other. We circle the disk. When standing at an angle, between head-on and behind, we can see a cyclone behind the disk, an umbilical cord to nowhere. But move a centimeter to front or back, right or left, and the disk is just a disk. Kano notes our findings and sketches the disk as it appears from the 2-D and 3-D angles. He mutters to himself about the possibilities.

Amina steps forward. "It gives off light!"

Light bounces violently around the warehouse, more like a siren than a watery reflection.

"It's not actually light," I say. "The disk, the mouth, is acting like a mirror and a prism, reflecting and refracting."

"But there's no light for it to reflect, and it's so bright in here."

I turn to my wife, who is so beautiful in her awe and confusion. I whisper to her. "Light from the other side."

"We'd only hypothesized about the principles of the mouth," Kano says. "This is spectacular."

We send a Goda through the Doorway. The Goda goes through for under a minute. We can't risk losing it. The Goda returns with video and sound and radiation levels and atmospheric readings. Kano and I review the data. A simple FireWire connection from Goda to computer, and we have seats in front to another world's show.

We continue reviewing while Amina does calculations—while she orders us lunch and then dinner. She tries to keep the guards outside and the delivery boy outside, but they see something, a shimmering, and Amina worries. We tell her it's okay.

"Can't the Goda somehow get telemetry?" she asks.

"Not until we know how the wormhole works."

"This Doorway," I emphasize. Kano's never been a fan of my terminology.

"And we can apply some information to see if it's Earth. But otherwise, we don't have any reference point except for stars."

"No stars on this video. Daylight."

"Can't you take EM readings?" Amina asks. "Then, you could at least look for Earth's EM signature."

She is brilliant. Still, we are hoping for the other side to be not Earth. I leave them for a walk, to figure some calculations. The wind here in Canada is different. It carries more, *can* carry more. The wind carries us—me, my shock and delight away, to the streets where life is Earth-life and where wind carries us to each other, together.

The video of Goda's first trip: A gray-green sky, perhaps because of sunrise or sunset. Tall tree without leaves or needles and mountains behind, rising like gods from the earth. We cannot see the ground from this vantage. Wind blows, and nothing moves. Everything is still and immobile, like the mountains. The mountains, frozen in prayer.

I walk, and I see why they say this is a bad neighborhood. All that I can see is rundown buildings, some stilled industry, but once I get a few blocks away, rundown houses. The weather is worse than I expected, especially for May, and I thought Madison was the end of that misery. I'm freezing my balls, and they might really fall off here in Canada.

I see an old woman smoking on her front porch. Her gloves have holes so her fingers poke through. Her hair is dark with a little white, and her boots don't match her robe, two different shades of pink. She seems sad, but then she spots me and becomes angry. "You smell American," she says, and laughs. "Why're you watching me? Don't you get enough movies in America?" I begin to tell her that I am a scientist doing important research that may one day make her country famous, but I know she won't understand.

I wish I'd brought my scarf. The wind blows so hard that my vision suffers. All around me, white and still I keep walking.

A long time ago, the universe began. A cat prowled in blackness, and its eyes caught some light. The reflection is the stars, and finally light and sky out of endless reflection. Then, hot breath. Fur is the earth. Blood, fire of the earth. Saliva, the ocean. The cat was gone.

I asked my mother, "Did the light kill him?"

She said the beginning itself is death.

I asked, "What religion is this story?"

She said all religions teach good stories. She said you may take stories from wherever you want. It's not stealing. She said you had to understand the difference between the prophet and religion. She said religions tell stories, and prophets speak truth. She said prophets come one after another, and you should always make sure your religion is the latest truth. She laughed at me, my confused eyes.

At the hotel, Amina is cooking again. Her vindaloo—with *no* potatoes. She asks me how long.

"Just a few more tests. It's a good sign the Goda can return."

"Do you remember after my parents died?" Amina asks, setting a plate down for me.

I don't answer. I shove food in.

"You promised I would never be alone."

"You'll have Kano."

"Kano is *your* friend, not mine."

"I'm coming back. Don't worry."

"If you don't, I'll come and get you."

I look at her slitted eyes. She's never mean, not really. Amina speaks her expectations and intentions clearly. She gets lonely, though. She said to me once that she has always been lonely.

"How will you come get me?" I grin my challenge at her.

She pulls back a bit, opens her mouth and closes it. Her eyes open up wide, and she says, "Do you think a woman, even an Indian woman, remains faithful to an absent husband in this twenty-first century?"

I met Amina two years before my mother died. We sat in the coffee shop. Kano had arranged our meeting, through what he called social networking. He knew I had a thing for Indian women.

The first thing Amina said to me was, "I was born in America, so if you're looking for a subservient foreign woman, you should leave now." I laughed, and she told me she'd heard about me, my fetish. I asked her what a fetish was, and Amina told me: "An obsession you cannot control." I told her this: what she called fetish, I could control. She asked me what I couldn't control. I told her nothing. I was in complete control. She smiled.

The next day as I approach the warehouse, Frusso is there. He and Kano are outside talking. As I approach, Frusso asks if there have been any more incidents. Kano says no, and Frusso leaves after giving his men strict instructions.

Kano is messy, like he's been in a fight. He falls into a chair and buries his face.

"What is it? Did the stranger come back?"

"No," he whispers. He points to his computer. He has been up sending the Goda through. He's tried different calibrations. Goda has been to many worlds!

I'm still, not breathing. I look through the video footage. Several worlds are blackness. Some are blackness and constellations we don't recognize. One is what must be fusion, heavy to light, from what we see and desire, CNO!

And then the habitable. Another is a brilliant blue ocean with endless archipelagos, with fog-horn music so loud. Another is rocks, but shining black, and a sky like cotton candy. Another is entirely flat, flat metal, and we can see movement of something—animals, people. And we can hear some sound, a siren sound with a melody. Another is desert, and Goda's vision is blurred by heat, but we can still see a storm on the horizon moving like a carnival ride.

Another is winter, simply, yet it is beautiful, too. There are so many pictures.

"I can't figure out how to access the same one twice," Kano says.

"Don't worry, friend," I say, smiling big. "We'll figure it out."

Kano and I work all day. He falls asleep in the early afternoon while I continue, alone. The calculations, the physics of it don't make sense. I know we're in uncharted territory, that negative energy hasn't been studied. We can create it but only fleetingly. Here today, gone in less than sixty seconds. As NE streams into existence we can only run quick tests. But we've run the tests, looked at variables. The details don't add up. There must be some logic.

But that is the logic, that we just don't know. We have something that is opposite to everything we know. So, we must opposite our tests. We must understand its role not in our world but in its own.

Observation: Alien comes to earth, and it cannot breathe. We try all the different gaseous mixtures, and the alien, cold and gray, still dies. Inside him, we find no lungs. The alien doesn't breathe. He produces his own food, rapid production of adipose tissue. He eats himself, and our atmosphere blocks this process. He was not suffocating, but starving.

We're testing for energy where the opposite of energy exists. What is the opposite of energy? Matter is another form of energy. The opposite must be—energy without matter, without the possibility of matter. This means we cannot test. This means, opposite isn't opposite but inestimable, unpredictable. The only solution is to open Schrödinger's box. We must not presume. I don't presume to be Dr. Pirvani, a scientist.

Amina is dreaming when I get back to the hotel. She sleeps before dinner. I see her eyes moving behind her lids, and her breathing, quick. Sweat on her nose. I wipe it away, and hope that for once, just once, she'll be happy to see me and not angry for my absence.

There's an envelope on the table:

> May 14, 2050
> You can't run. I know where you are. Were. Time is a lonely mistress. You can't keep me away.
> Let me tell you a story, about a tiger. He looked out at the universe, and his eyes reflected some light. In the end, the tiger was no more, but his reflection, the universe continued. All scientists should understand.
> —Zeroth

How did he find me? I am sweating like a glacier. Is this the right idiom?

A long time ago, I imagined myself a prince. I slew the dragon, but the dragon returned to life. I killed him again and again. I named him Goda because he was like Yoda in *Star Wars*— moving out of order, backwards, from death to life.

∿

For our anniversary dinner, we eat Chinese food. Except for her own cooking, it's Amina's favorite. She says it's her American pleasure even in Canada. Her parents never let her eat all of this bad Americanized fast food and takeout.

We sit in the small Chinese restaurant, sipping tea. There is a familiar smell of ginger and the odd smell of licorice. All around us are paintings of words. Ideograms, Amina tells me. Word-pictures, embellished. Who decorates their words?

Amina sips her tea and says, "I feel so very British. I should go forth and colonize."

"Tea doesn't belong to them."

"Ah, but it does," she says. "Once you have made one claim to ownership, you have made many."

"Can we talk about something nice and simple?" I ask. Her mouth is full of smart things, but tonight, I just want us to sit across from each other and say, "I love you" and, "I love you, too."

"The man who wants to change the world—no, many worlds—wants nice and simple? Did you ever think that I was nice and simple?"

"I think your hair is nice and simple," I say. A joke? I'm not sure, but I smile and laugh anyway. Amina stares at me, at crazy me. Then, she laughs, too, and the night moves forward with nice and simple conversations about old friends, that party from years ago, baby names, flowers (lily vs. orchid), and how we need a new car.

I decide not to tell Amina about the letter. My present for this day will be keeping my secret.

My father once said, "Would you like to take this book?" Which? *The Space Child's Guide to Mother Goose*. I said no. I am a scientist, I told him. Children's stories do nothing for me. He reminds me of Kip, Pee Wee and the Mother Thing. I tell him that I'm too old.

৵৵

And here is the next letter. This morning Kano found it outside the warehouse, taped to the Doorway. The guards saw nothing.

> May 15, 2050
> Do you remember?
> "There was an old man in a Time Machine
> Who borrowed Tuesday all painted green.
> His pockets with rockets he used to jam
> And he said, 'I have think, so I cannot am!'"
> Yes, you remember. Please go home to your dear wife, Amina. I will be forced to stop you.
> —Zeroth

"What is this?" Kano asks, reading the letter. "He's followed you?"

"Yes," I say, "but I think it's more than that. I think he *knows* Amina."

"Knows her?" Kano asks. "She isn't having an affair, Amir."

"I know, but he keeps writing to me about her."

"Don't you see?" Kano asks.

"See what?"

He turns away and lifts his head to the sky. "I can't. You'll see, in time, but if I say something, who knows?"

"Are you sleeping with my wife?"

Kano laughs and laughs. I remember silly Kano. I believe he is not with Amina, yet laughter is no medicine.

When I was a child, I loved my mother. My friends were small. *Few.* A boy who loved baseball lived down the street. He wanted to be my friend. He kept coming by our house to see if I could come out and play. I never did, until one day, shortly after my father died, when I was feeling *gamkeen.* The boy taught me to throw with two fingers. We ran, flew through red dirt. This kid, the kid who loved baseball, said that he had always wanted a brown friend. I told him that Mars was red from iron oxide.

The baseball kid said we could talk about colors all day long. Then, he threw a ball to me. I caught it! Red dust, clay, not on Mars, came up from my glove, and the baseball kid was still there.

He was my first friend. He told me to shut up and throw, run—*move*. He told me to look at him when he talked.

Five years later, he moved away, and he said goodbye like a real goodbye. But I had his new address and wrote him. I wrote him until I was sixteen and moved to MIT. I wanted to miss the baseball kid more, but I really only missed sun and earth, movement. Like a ball that curves.

At MIT, I saw Kano. He never told me to shut up. We moved around the lab. I watched Kano move, his arms, gesturing, and his eyes. Kano, gin-and-tonic and red-face, sneaky, and math whiz, like Fermat—and Kano who always told me the truth, though he always laughed and winked.

V.

Time to move. We've made a small NE emitter—travel-size, Kano says. It doesn't have as much power and has to rely on a battery. The travel-size looks like a sighting telescope that sailors would use to spot land. Land ho!

We're ready, but we want to stay here, on the edge of hope. Kano and I are brave, though. We make the decision. I move toward the darkness.

I am still with light of blue purple yellow white racing toward me. Catch it!

A cry in the distance, and I think of my son. The cry is me. I cry into dirt. The pressure around me threatens my body and my mind. My thoughts slow with thick dirt. I inhale and nothing happens. Chest is heavy like weight of, like density of atomic element number—number—K for Kano. No, Kano is a person. The dirt is intense heat and still dark. No light anywhere. It's not the ground, not what we walk on. I'm in it, and I'm not buried because there's no box and no looseness. Inexplicable. Densely packed earth and still alive. It is so *tarik*.

A forest. I'm in a forest. Slowly, light shines in my face. Slowly, I know that I went to the wrong place, that the Doorway redirected me, Doorway/operator of the Universe. My call is forwarded.

I check my body, and the NE emitter is still here, attached to my chest. All around, a true cold. The sky is bright and dark together, circles like eclipses dotting the sky. I move through, and take Goda from my pocket. He buzzes in the air, and I say, "Collect. Fifty yards." And he is off, a dog fetching wood for its master.

The light goes, and I'm cold again, colder than I was in the dirt. The dirt has an aroma of food, like popcorn. I cup some in my hand and look very closely. For a moment, I think it moves, the dirt. But I look again, and it's dirt, motionless. I try to start a fire with the fibrous plants, which grow large like trees, but they melt to white without flames. The smell is of burnt hair.

With the dotted-spotted sky, I don't know what days are, not really. Are the dark spots like clouds? I sleep, and Goda's timer says I sleep for ten hours at a time. After what Goda says is two days, I grow very hungry. I try to eat the plants-like-trees, but my teeth cannot get through. I review Goda's footage and see only these for miles.

I will return to Canada. This is nothing. The NE emitter still has a lot of power.

This is Earth! And the sky, it is Edmonton, but I'm in woods. I know it is Edmonton from that wind, that wind which carries so much. I must have fallen far from the Warehouse. When I return, Amina will kiss me like Greta Garbo, and Kano will have outsmarted the stranger. I will have gun and smoking—tell them of my adventures in Monument Valley.

I move, and my hunger takes me down. The wind blows my hungry body to the ground, dirt and snow mixed. I lie there for sleep, a bone-bag.

Bright sky like a field of white grass. Clouds zooming by and back. I move through the foliage, toward sound.

A highway and orange cones and signs warning of construction workers. I know this highway. I-94, and a home that I don't want. This isn't Edmonton. I am home: Madison, WI.

VI.

People say, "Do you remember where you were when _____?" I remember. Here I am, not outside of time but twice in it. First Me and Second Me. Time instead of Space. I have no power. You can conquer places and not time. I remember where I was when I opened the newspaper and realized I was twenty-five years old and ten years old, together. Paradox is only paradox if you get philosophical. Science allows for paradox, but my heart, my heart—with my heart, I could barely allow it. My Amina was years away.

Where I was: an old gas station with an old attendant. The newspaper said November 11, 2034. The newspaper said, "You must wait for the world to catch you." *Sabr* and *sabr*. How does a man wait for the world? I became like a child, a child of the small and familiar, the *stories*.

Here is a famous story. Rostam had to fight for the king. Rostam must kill Div-e Sefid, the white demon. Div-e Sefid was tall and white but white that wasn't clean. The great *div* kidnapped the king and blinded him and his men. Rostam had seven quests, and the last is for the king.

They fought a mighty battle stirring up a mighty wind. Div-e

Sefid was winning, and he stopped to laugh. As he laughed with his great white chest stuck out, Rostam gathered strength and put a spear in the great demon. As he died, Div-e Sefid said he would return and fight Rostam again.

Rostam used the demon's blood to heal the blindness. He also took the demon's helmet and wore it always.

Years later, Div-e Sefid's son, Shabrang came to fight Rostam. Shabrang was dark as night, black without any moon and stars. Rostam won.

Rostam is hero of Iran. He won many battles, but in the end he lost much. He was revered but envied. He was a hero but could never stop. Rostam killed his own son, though by accident.

I rented an apartment. I ate cheap steak that smelled of fat and heat and musk of animal. I slept on the floor and thought in a chair. I watched the sun move across the sky—but only on days when the white haze allowed.

Tarzan didn't really get the girl. He had to work hard and turn away from everything he had known and loved. Tarzan had to leave the jungle to get Jane.

Tarzan didn't know who he was, but it turned out he was rich! But Jane loved him anyway.

In the beginning, Jane was afraid of him. She loved him, but she was afraid of him. She wondered, could she love what she feared? I want to tell Jane that you can only love what you fear, but I think she figured it out.

And with his Jane, Tarzan returned to the Africa. There was no peaceful happy after, for these two were adventurers. I will never forget Tarzan in Pellucidar. Oh, Pellucidar, where there is only now and no time because the sun doesn't set and the horizon doesn't exist. The world is a circle.

I thought about Thorne. I used to be a Thorne purist. Kip Thorne would say this wasn't possible. But I'm here, in an

impossibility, a dream, a closed time curve. Kip Thorne once
said, "The right answer is seldom as important as the right
question." Well, where am I, Mr. Thorne?

Zah-re-mar, the snake, moves like a thief. The first snake ever
created ate up all the sand in the world. The sand gave away its
movement. But then, without the sand, the snake was nothing.
The snake couldn't move at all.

A tiger and a bear fought in the middle of a great forest.
Very well, a tiger and a bear fought in the middle of a great
forest.

My father and I read science fiction. We were scientists. My
mother read along with us, but she never said much about these
stories.

Then, when I was in high school, my mother told me
about Demonbot. I was so much older, too old for stories,
but she insisted. She said that a great scientist had invented
a robot and left out the rule of Zeroth. The robot killed the
man who was trying to stop the mad scientist from blowing
up the moon. Then, the oceans rose up and swallowed all
men. The robots survived but were left all alone. My mother
said to always remember the Zeroth law, the greater good.
She said if you were left all alone, the world would be a
watery grave, no peace.

I grew tired of drywall and silence. And because I had nothing
but stories, I went back to find my parents and First Me, in
Texas. I watched. Then, I decided to get a job with the
aeronautics company so that I could work beside my father. I
stayed with my father until he died.

At the aeronautics company, I was a lab rat and not a scientist.
I was one of three assistants to my father. I worked as I should.
I watched my father work. He never went home, and this time

round, I knew what he was doing. But his discovery, it was mediocre and would only change the world in wartime.

> Old Mother Goose,
> When she wanted to wander,
> Would ride through the air
> On a very fine gander.
> Jack's mother came in,
> And caught the goose soon,
> And mounting its back,
> Flew up to the moon.

A few months before my father's death, he asked me if I'd ever been in love. I told him that I had always been in love. He didn't understand. I told him that I had always known who I would love. He didn't understand, so I told him that love was like memory. His gray hair gripped in his hand. He asked me how to ask a woman's forgiveness. I told him to ask her. I told him to speak, to move. He nodded.

The seven valleys. The first six are Search, Love, Knowledge, Unity, Contentment, and Wonderment. The seventh is True Poverty and Absolute Nothingness. Baha'u'llah says, "These journeys have no visible ending in the world of time, but the severed wayfarer—if invisible confirmation descend upon him and the Guardian of the Cause assist him—may cross these seven stages in seven steps, nay rather in seven breaths, nay rather in a single breath, if God will and desire it." I am in the first valley, and my own desire is great. I wish to reach the lined finish, the finish lined with silver.

Once, just once, my father told me a story. He said that as a child he had believed in many things. He said his own father was a religious man, who had given a great deal to the Baha'i Faith. He asked me if I knew about that religion, and I said yes.

He said his father had sacrificed his own family's wealth. He said his father had given him no money to come to America. He said he had never spoken to his own son about his grandfather. He'd said his father was killed a long time ago, in an accident.

I asked my father why he hated his father so much. He said, "He gave me nothing. I don't hate him. I feel nothing for the man who gave me nothing."

"And what have you done for your own son?" I asked.

"I read to him until he got too smart for that. I smile at him. I play with his hair, like this," he said, and then he tousled my hair, like a coach would, I think.

I smiled at my father. I asked, "Do you think that he'll remember?"

The alien is a robot, and his blood begins to boil. We must give him some hugs.

Two years, we worked together. I watched him in the lab. Sometimes, he would drink in the lab. His co-workers were his friends. They played pranks on each other. Once, my father opened a drawer and a slew of false snakes jumped out at him.

It was good to see him laugh.

I was still outside the room when my mother said goodbye, when she was yelling at him, my father. My younger self, too. I watched my younger self, but I stayed away, not wanting to solve the mystery of what my parents said in my father's last moments.

I went back into the room once they had left.

"Do you want me to tell them anything after you're gone?" I asked.

My father said, "They should know my sacrifice already. They should know and always be angry."

"Anger fades like everything else," I said.

He laughed.

He had two buckets in this room, one for piss and shit and another for vomit. His vomit was black, a pure black of space. It was thick. I felt glad I couldn't smell it.

The black bile, one of the four humors. Oh, my father's sadness. He hid his sadness.

Then later, my father said, "Go to, go to." He threw up again. He looked up at me with pleading. He said, "Go to." I told him I was a scientist, and I would not leave. He just kept repeating, "Go to." In the moment, I heard *goda*. Perhaps, I heard everything wrong. And how did my First Me also take that mishearing and remember it? Perhaps, I ruined the space-time of consciousness. Memory is future tense?

And yes, I did leave. I left my father. I went to, went to, went to. Conjugated his death. My second time, my Second Self tries to learn English right.

VII.

I called Kano too soon, when the ideas of the Doorway were just beginning for us, but I was lonely. I had to call Kano, my *baradar*, so I bought a cell phone. I called Kano, but his cell number wasn't the same. I forgot. So, I called Transportech, and they left him my number. I told them I'm a recruiter for the Defense Department.

"Is this a new number?" Kano asked.

"I'm not your Amir," I said. "I'm Amir from fifteen years before, from fifteen years later."

"What?" Kano asked, and he laughed. "Your games." I said nothing, and then, I heard him inhale. "So," he said, "it works but not as we'd expected."

"Yes, and we cannot tell your First Me."

"But that means you just disappear."

"Perhaps not."

"What are you going to do?"

"I'm not sure yet," I said. "But I cannot keep in touch. You must simply remember that when the time comes, take care of Amina."

Kano and I talked about how he could keep the two me's separate. We decided not to talk any more. The larger issue was how to control him, to keep him from planning to take over my life. He asked questions: "Where should I take Amina after you disappear? Back to Madison? Should I stay with her?" He scared me with his questions. I didn't want Amina to be alone, and all she knew was Kano. She'd never had that many friends. Would she marry Kano because he was my friend, or would she really love him?

I read some poems to try to learn English. I read about ice cream and fire and ice. I read about a wasted land, and I know this word "Shantih" somehow, though I'm not sure why my wife would ever say it. There is a tiger somewhere, burning bright.

My mother dies again, twice, as my father did. My mother flies up to the moon.

I waited for years. Bad food and bad movies—bad movies about the future. Finally, 2049, and I know what I have done, but what have I done? I'm at home, at our old house. I hold her panties in my hand, stolen from my own dryer—because so it was written, as those Christians say. They smell clean.

As I write letters to First Me, I wonder if this is how my mother felt: like a god. The snow piles on outside. I stay warm and write with as perfect English as I can. I try to scare with sex.

2049, and here is a pretty picture. Here is Amina, through the window, making American cherry pie. She is smaller but with our son. She sweats a little, on her nose. I'm outside of my old house in Madison, in a gathering of trees, within view of my old home, a kitchen window. Later in the night, I see myself, First Me. Tonight, I will have my pie and eat it, too.

I know what I have done, but I wonder still: "What have I done?" And the echo: "Do I dare?"

৵৵

At the local library. Muspell was first. Fire, then ice. It is a very long poem.

In my old home, I remember. We are away that night, at a friend's house. Inside, I am more courageous than before. I go through clothes in the closet. I go into the bathroom. Her perfume, like sun through clouds. Then, I look up, at myself. I'm old, a withering old man trying to save the world by following the rules, by allowing the future that the past declares.

Downstairs, I find the sonogram. I find the cherry pie—delicious, so sweet, and so warm. I take them both.

Outside in the gathering trees, I eat and blood-red, damn spot on my hands. I haunt myself.

When they leave for Canada, I leave, too. I drive through the cold wet. Water sprays up around my car, and I look at the world through drops of rain. The world is a mosaic of white and gray, some brown.

I practice speaking slowly, properly. I recite Shakespeare sonnets I have memorized. No more Disney movies. I have grown up!

I find a room, less expensive, in the Westin. I work on letters. I think "Dear Abby"—and how those Americans take advice from someone they've never met. I think to write in headlines: "Man Sent Back in Time, Reunited with his Wife." I think how I never learn English like I should. I read English-learning books, and also poetry. I feel hopeless. Words fly away.

I write a million letters. I read poetry. I think and wonder too much. If she will understand my disappearance, if Kano will try to kiss her, if she will name the child after me once I'm gone, if she will tell him about my genius, if she will tell him the stories. But I have to keep it simple. I have to be dangerous. *Scary*. Mystery must remain on my side.

ৼৣৢঌ

Amina cooks tonight, and as I look up at the balcony, I don't
see stars but her hair in the winter wind. Down, down, down, a
note for me. An airplane bringing to me—math. Her math, and
the unknown variables. She was right. We didn't account for
enough. We forgot about uncertainty. We forgot about time.

In the cold night, I look up and remember. In the cold night,
I exhale into this world, and see the proof of my existence,
though it should be impossible for one man to be in two places.
In the cold night, I know that we are not the same man, that he
is not a vision of my youth any more than I am. We are enemies
now. I reason that I must do what he did not do so that he will
not do what I did. I consider the options, the consequences. I
accept all risk. I weigh the risk, and it tips the scales. But still.

An abstract:

A Doorway leads to difference. In terms of space-time, we
cannot quantify or predict the destination. The only thing is to
go, go to. After, we will know.

A transversable wormhole can be induced by negative energy.
Due to the instability of negative energy, in terms of our own
understanding of quantum physics, the pathway is impossible to
predict. While maintaining variables pertaining to negative energy
and our own uniquely constructed negative energy emitter, we find
it nearly impossible to open Doorways to the same destination.
However, we hypothesize that from the other side of the Doorway,
what we will call side D (for destination), we can immediately direct
the same frequency and intensity of negative energy and return to
the origin (O). Utilizing a Goda, a self-suspending robotics device,
we have found this to be possible in several trials. Thus, we
hypothesize the likelihood of two-way transversable wormholes,
depending upon entry, or travel, and not induction.

Who would believe my story? I attack the warehouse, shoot through
the sunlit window. I shoot the sun. I'm the nothing that is.

༆

I wait, to obey the timeline. Then, I play the role of delivery boy, dress up as if for a play with clothes and hair and mustache.

I see the Doorway when it first opens up, though Amina tries to block my view. I laugh and say, "This is some crazy setup you've got here!"

I poisoned the food with clonazepam.

After about an hour, I return. Frusso and his men sleep. Kano and Amina asleep. I wonder where First Me is. I cannot wait, risk everything. I take the NE emitter. I bash it and bash it and bash it. I take the computer and I tear it up. This will be a huge delay, and after my son is born, First Me won't want to leave anyway.

I hear yelling, and the large warehouse Doorway screams, too. I listen to First Me call for Amina. When First Me approaches, I hit him hard on the head. There is a little blood. In panic, I wonder if I have killed myself, if I should. But the scientist I am says, "No, First Me is fine. If he weren't, you'd disappear." It's not a movie, though. Science allows for paradox. Then, I wonder if stories aren't true, if science isn't a story. The man lies on the floor, blood from his ears and so bright. He is young and even now seems full of life. His hair has color, his skin, even his blood.

VIII.

The *div* wasn't always assumed a demon. Before Zoroaster and one god, the *div* was just a god who didn't know how to discern truth from lie—or a god who *chose* not to discern truth from lie. The *div* was a trickster but mostly just a survivor. It's confusing. My mother told me a story about the *div* stealing children. She said the *div* could steal children because children loved the *div*. So why is this bad? Wouldn't children be happy with someone they loved?

I feel glory. After so many years, to know that it's over, that I have saved myself. I feel fear, too. I need to see that First Me is okay. I've done this all for him.

I change my clothes and wait outside. The sleeping awake. First Me has trouble walking, and Amina and Kano hold him up. Just by the car, he melts to the ground. Amina cries and yells. I follow them to the hospital.

I pull at my hat, and watch as Kano gently touches Amina's arm. The doctor comes to say that he thinks First Me just has a concussion.

Amina says, "Are you sure?"

They must run more tests. The doctor leaves.

Amina says, "Kano, who did this? Why?"

Kano shakes his head. "Maybe Transportech."

I speed by them, and behind me, Kano says, "What's that smell?"

Does he know me? I want to say, "Old friend, it's done. Our secret is over." Does he realize? Kano perhaps never thought what I would do. Perhaps he has forgotten Second Me.

Outside, Canada is white and still. My heart is like a mountain, frozen in prayer. A prayer I remember: "Is there any remover of difficulties, save God? Say: Praised be God! He is God! All are his servants, and all abide by his bidding!"

Another prayer: *Please let me live. Please let me live. Please let me live.*

IX.

Here is a famous poem about the seven ages of man. I am at the end of second childhood and oblivion. I am at the end with nothing. Without. I think this Shakespeare knew about getting old before your time, about waiting too long. My hair has grown gray, and my skin wrinkles like the plum so cold and delicious. My eyes have filled with sadness. *Ghadim.*

First Me died—of skull fracture, swelling, brain death—but I'm still here. I don't know if I died on my own or if Amina took me off life support. I suppose it doesn't matter. I died. I die. But I am still here. It is a study in MWI, perhaps. I think of John Archibald Wheeler and of Schrödinger and his cat. I am the wavelength, the cat. I am hungry in a box of time, my tongue killed by curiosity.

Kano has taken care of Amina. They are married. She named my son after me, so Kano has a new me, a Third Me. Third Me is like Kano, laughing and joking. Sly, like a fox. That's an idiom I never understood. The fox only does what he must to survive. Human slyness is less true than that. Maybe I still don't understand English.

At the funeral for First Me, I stood apart from the group. I stood in sunshine and nicely cut grass. I lay in a dark box. Here I am, dead.

I wore sunglasses and a hat. Disguised, but halfway through the service, I saw Kano staring at me. He stared at me until the funeral was over. I wanted to hug my friend, but I was also frightened of him.

I returned to Wisconsin. I got a job at that old gas station. If I wasn't working, I stayed home and read. I read big books like *The Divine Comedy* and *Moby Dick*. I tried to do more than understand English. I tried to understand what Americans valued so that I could understand my wife. The great American novel is always an untold story that is too long. What Americans value is justice, the cowboy—in the end the "right" winning. We all get what we have coming, even if it's ourselves.

For years, I thought of ways to get close to my son, to become his tutor, baseball coach, piano teacher. I remained fearful. Kano has done as I asked and taken care of Amina. She seems happy, and so does Third Me. I'm fearful of ruining all of that. Or that's what I tell myself. I tell myself stories that may be true. Third Me looks a great deal like Kano.

The stories allow me to leave. Are all stories lies? What is it that I wanted to save? A marriage or a scientist? I can leave now, without the call of home. Nowhere to return. Point of. Home again. I read a poem: "Home's the place we head for in our sleep."

X.

I cannot remember the stories any more. A long, long time ago and a land far, far away. I remember vaguely the American fairy tales. My mother never read these to me, but instead teachers at school. American fairy tales are so neat. Long, long ago—so that we cannot know. Far, far away—so that we cannot reach. My mother's stories always seemed to be there before me, to be a magic that was real.

Yesterday, I saw my son outside playing. He ran like wind. He stopped a great deal, to turn and gaze at the gathering trees, at me. He didn't see me, I don't think. He saw maybe some movement? He seems like something my mind made up. He seems like magic. I won't ask about how the trick does.

They named my son Amir.

At my mother's grave now. I stand very, very still. I don't expect to hear a story. I listen for the memories from my other selves, who encode memories from innumerable times. I live forever. I remember before and before things happen. I remember the snow of my death.

My NE emitter still works after all these years. I found it quite easy to charge it. I'm afraid to go through. But I don't like feeling the pressure of time. My bones creak and are returning to dust. Is this right? I remember my old life. I remember Amina's nose with a drop of sweat, Kano's wink, and a letter about snow. But I remember more than that.

If I didn't know how everything ended, I could be a scientist.

Her grave is simple. A gray stone that says "Dear Mother of Amir. A woman of strength and love." I place my flowers and walk away, down the dirt road, feeling no better for having come. Why must we come to the grave? Doesn't memory serve well enough?

I remember my mother on a hot August day. She was young, and she wore shorts. She sat in a chair outside with me. We were grilling, though I was too young to help. When she got up, the vinyl clung to her skin, making a sucking sound. Quick sand. Tarzan escaped. My mother said, "Amir, tell me a story." And I did. I told her about coming back home. I told her about Tarzan, clowns, ice. I told her about ice that was calm and ice that was furious. She placed an ice cube on my forehead and told me that I would grow up to be a crazy man. She blew on the first done kebob and placed it gently on my tongue. She told me about the demon that would steal it from me if I didn't eat it right away. The sunlight fell down. The air became thick like a monster. The sounds of evening lulled me to insanity. Again home, *div* from time beginning. Crazy in love.

In the Middle
of Many Mountains

I want to tell you the story of my mother's death, but I'm not sure we're ready. The story begins far away, in Nayriz, a city in the middle of many mountains that my mother always said was similar in appearance and climate to Tucson, Arizona. I've never been to Nayriz or Tucson. My mother always said that in Nayriz when it was summer, the heat burned everything it touched and everything touched burned like the heat. Seems reasonable enough.

Home now, after a long while. I drive up—see my house, my mother, not directly but through the infrared of my stars. Heat is in the kitchen and heat is in my mother's broken eyes. Young holly trees at the head of the driveway bend under the weight of berries. Bark peeling off, soft to the touch. My mother's skin feels just so, and as I hug her, I count her vertebrae, tickling her spine to make sure she will not die in my arms.

The sprinkler sprays us as we move towards the house. The sky is murky.

Remember: astronomy, my stars are left alone, left behind. The IRT is of no use here. Science will not tell the story, my younger teenage sister's almost-death which is my mother's death.

My sister, she wouldn't eat. And now she has run away like a child. I'll try to tell you more.

The search for my sister begins with a large midday meal that might put you to sleep. *Lubia polow.* Green beans, tomatoes, and chicken with rice. Seasoned with cinnamon. *Khoresh-e qeymeh.* Split yellow chickpeas, tomatoes, and fried potato strips on top. Seasoned with turmeric. *Kalam polow.* Cabbage, onions, lentil beans, and small meatballs with rice. Seasoned with cumin and turmeric. *Lozeh badam.* Peeled and ground almonds, sugar and rose water. Seasoned with cardamom. Blended into a sweet mixture, then shaped like stars. When she was younger, my mother's mother used to tell her not to eat too many candies because eating stars, like wishing on them, was dangerous.

My mother has laid out the table in such splendor, but she has to squint at silverware before we begin. And we must begin before we can find my sister.

My sister ran away a few days ago. She just graduated high school.

My mother thinks Marjan ran away because our father left in December. This might be so. I wonder if Marjan is truly upset or if she is angry because there is no battle over her. Maybe my sister wishes she were younger so there would be something at stake: her whole life. So people couldn't say, *At least the girls were grown up when it happened.*

When my mother called last week, I promised her I would find Marjan.

"Eat more," my mother says.

"We should talk," I say, thinking of Marjan.

"No, eat more."

My mother eats with her face close to the plate. Behind her on the wall, a still-life of African violets, hanging crookedly. On the table, brass candelabras, candles unlit.

႞ఎఎ

My mother lived a really long time. Too long, and in the end, she was blind and talking like Tiresias. She said, "Your father wasn't really your father," and, "You don't know your family." But this isn't the right beginning.

After eating, I call Marjan and leave a message telling her that Mother is wasting her eyes on crying. I search Marjan's room. Under the bed, I find an ankle bracelet with letters strung together: *Summer Fun*. In the back of her nightstand drawer, I find a poem about snakes in desert sand. On the bookshelf, all of my father's books. Taped to the back of her standing mirror, I find our father's wedding ring. On the wall, there is a framed star chart of the Northern Hemisphere that I gave her for her sixteenth birthday.

I'll have to tell you about my American father leaving my mother for an intellectual companion. A woman whose hair wasn't so dark as my mother's, who knew more than stories and could navigate metaphysical questions, the notion of your father not being your father or of your love not being your love.

During the Christmas holiday weekend, he told my mother he was leaving. I hid in the kitchen, filled with real Persian stews and frozen American pies, apple and pumpkin. My mother loves the frozen American pies.

My father avoided all intellectual language, and in fact, spoke to my mother the way he'd been speaking to her for the past twenty-five years, like a child who didn't understand.

"This isn't working," he said, gesturing at the entire living room, the house. "This isn't working. Not working."

But my mother was an adult who didn't quite understand English, a difference that should have been honored.

After he left, I went into the living room with a piece of pumpkin pie for my mother. Her favorite.

She didn't cry. She looked at me and said, "I can't tell my mother. She's too old to handle this."

Later that week, my father called to say that we could get rid of all of his stuff. He surprised us by leaving all of his books. *The Divine Comedy.* The stars are not so holy. A wheel turned evenly? This isn't my universe.

I went through most of the books, poking holes through the parched pages with my fingernails. A soft clicking sound, a book gnawed upon. So easy to destroy old things.

Marjan yelled when she saw what I'd done to the books. She took them, all of them.

My mother was brave. She didn't cry about the divorce for almost one year. That's why her eyes went bad. Go ahead, look directly at the sun.

Marjan is at the Motel 6 on Cheatham St. I find her there, eating cheese and crackers.

"I can't take care of her," my sister says.

"I don't understand," I say. "You can leave."

"I can't," she says. "He made that impossible. She'll be all alone. She won't have anyone to talk to."

The room smells like bleach, and my sister, she doesn't smell at all. She is a dark-haired, dark-skinned girl who looks like my mother. Marjan sits Indian style with crumbs all around. There will be some proof that she was here.

"I need you to help me," Marjan says, "but you're not going to like it. You won't want to hear."

I don't want to see. Her, barely there, five-year-old limbs stretched out to form an adult. We are always playing with dolls. If I listen to her, will I go blind?

And maybe this is how the story begins—in Farsi, a language I don't quite understand. *Jan* for "dear," *khub* for "good," *bala* for "yes," *che* for "what." And *zah-re-mar*, "poison of the snake." Who is the betrayer?

༄༅

At home, my mother wants to know where I've been, and I tell her that I had to go see about a star, a brown dwarf that my colleagues located. My mother says that it sounds like a fairytale. She asks me which American fairytale has dwarfs in it.

For the afternoon, we sit outside on the deck to work with the pomegranates. We're making more food for tonight—in case Marjan comes home. We should all eat together.

I hold a bowl for the fleshy seeds. On the ground, we have a plastic bag for the skin and hollowed pith. She is showing me how to make one of my favorite stews. My mother insists she must teach me how to remove the seeds completely from the pith because the pith is bitter. No art is involved in removing the seeds. I don't really need a lesson.

The oak tree. I sit in its shade, but my mother stands in the summer sun. Perhaps the sun doesn't bother her so much anymore. She stands in front of me. The pomegranate juice sprays into my eyes and onto my clothes. She laughs at me because she knew that this would happen. My mother warned me before we started, and I took her advice—wear old clothes and wipe the juice out of my eyes quickly. I never received the usual motherly advice. In elementary school, my classmates had sun-staring contests during recess. I always won. At a price, I'm sure.

My mother moves closer to read my old t-shirt. "Is that a beer bottle on your shirt?" she asks.

"Yes," I say. I almost tell her that it belonged to someone else, that the shirt was free, that beer helps me sleep. Lies are a habit, but I'm too old for all of this.

"Oh," she says, "I need you to write a letter for me. Perry Ellis didn't refund all of my money for the perfume."

Beer, perfume. We should get rid of the indulgences. Is that the connection? Or is it simpler? Bottles. Perhaps, it's even simpler.

"Be careful," my mother says, as she gets sprayed. She laughs, and the wind carries that music upwards with the heat. The deck is stained with blood.

In Hawaii, life goes on without me. I have left my observatory, my stars behind. They continue to be born, in dust and particle cloud and muck of space—their red-hot secret safe from me. And the Universe expands until everything is old and its newness, its beginning, becomes a red that only I could see, if I were there.

I always tell my students that infrared astronomy is about seeing what the very young and the very old do not want you to see. We are caretakers, I tell them.

Before we were born, my father owned a telescope. On boring Michigan nights, he stargazed. He also imagined stories to go along with the lights that he saw in the sky. When we were kids, he told us these stories at night. He told us of a planet where creatures looked like gargoyles and built their castles on the side of sharp, smooth cliffs. A desert planet. He told us of another planet where creatures could be male or female or nothing. A winter planet. Later, I found his stories in books. The worst sort of lie.

We blend the pomegranate seeds, then strain the juice.

"You should tell me your recipes," I say, "so I'll know what to do when you stop cooking."

"Whenever you come home, I'll cook for you." She refills the saltshaker. "Besides, you don't have the patience."

"I do. I have a lot of patience."

"Will you write that letter for me today?" she asks.

My mother just can't wait for words. She has a professional way of speaking that she uses with me when she's not tired, but she cannot write legibly or type. She is always dictating to someone. When she dictated to my father, he changed her words entirely, made them excessively formal. I wonder if I have the patience to listen to her, to fix her words.

❧

Marjan is sick with anorexia. The next time I visit her at the motel, she tells me how to save her. I insist on her coming home.

"No," she says. "There's too much food."

The room is so neat. Today, the scent of lemon.

"I don't want you to go," I say.

"I have to," she says, playing with the rubber bands on her wrist. "It's the best facility, and my college money will cover it. It all makes sense."

"You have to tell her."

"No, don't tell her anything," Marjan says.

I cannot understand silence, but I know that I'll go home and stuff my mouth with food.

The story ends with me crying as a grown woman. The one time my mother actually held me as a grownup. That one time, she held me, her body already small from her own grief. They say caffeine sucks calcium out of your bones. It's much worse with sadness. And we waste away.

Don't worry. There is an ending after this one.

My father fell in love quickly, I think. He left so quickly.

Right after, we rarely talked on the phone. About a month later, though, he came to visit me in Hawaii, with his new lover, but made me promise not to tell Marjan or my mother.

My father said to me, "I always think of things to tell you, but then I can't remember."

The truth, but I wished he would lie to me, too.

My sister has been institutionalized, and my mother is going blind. My mother needs several substantial eye surgeries, so I've moved home to be with her. You see, my mother is afraid to be put to sleep, for she might never wake up.

I took a sabbatical from the University. I told them all that I would be back soon.

But I know I might never leave here.

Marjan was my secret first, then our secret. I had to tell her, you see.

"She doesn't like my food anymore?" my mother asked.

"She's just angry," I said. "She needs to be alone."

"Will you write a letter to her for me?"

And I did. I wrote Marjan two letters, one from me and one from my mother.

My father and I still talk once a week. I will not tell him where Marjan really is.

So, have I kept her secret?

In November, a letter from my father arrives. I make my mother open it. The letter from my father reads as if from a stranger. The letter is formal. He declares his intention to marry again and be separated from my mother "in every respect."

My mother reads the letter out loud to me with the pace and care of a child. I already knew this was the end.

She asks me what the letter means. "How is this different from what's already going on? I thought we were divorced."

"No," I say, "you're just separated. You have to sign papers to be legally divorced."

The next morning before she goes in for surgery, she says, "I hope I die. It would serve him right." She wipes her tears away. "And your sister." But I'm not sure that my sister won't die first.

When I was eight, my mother asked me to write her a letter to Belk. Her store credit card had appeared with her first name misspelled. She couldn't have them change it unless they had a written and signed request. Usually, my father did this sort of chore. He was busy, though, and my mother knew I was old enough to compose a letter.

She wanted the letter to be polite. She dictated to me, emphasizing words that indicated humility and precursory appreciation. Instead, I relayed outrage. I claimed that in Persian culture to misspell someone's name was tantamount to calling the person weak. I assured the managers of Belk that my mother was not weak. She would live forever and lay waste to their empire. And could they mail a new card within the next seven to ten business days?

I say that my sister stopped eating because that's the common way of understanding anorexia. What it really means is that you don't love the people around you any more, and you punish yourself for it. This isn't weakness.

I knew it was happening. She came to visit me before it got bad, before she ran away from home. I should have known. She wanted frozen yogurt for lunch. She asked me to borrow clothes that were too big for her. She fell asleep at eight o'clock. She dreamt of mountains.

Marjan calls me a few times. She says, "I think snow is like the bark of our holly trees and like the places on TV." She says, "I beat Mark in chess today. But he taught me how, so it doesn't count." She says, "If I die, put a picture of a constellation on my marker. Cassiopeia." She says, "I think you know me. I think I'm still the same." She says, "I miss you."

My father described movement in the poetry he wrote as a child. When he lived on the shore of Lake Michigan, he noted the patterns of the water's movement, how every few minutes you could expect an eighth-note rhythm to emerge. According to my father, the quickening was a watery joy, a jazz attack.

Later, he lived in Oklahoma, landlocked. Then, he described the clouds. To describe the sky, though, he didn't use music or art or love. He used scientific names for cloud types—a sort of truth, I suppose. He wrote academic articles for his high school paper about cloud formations. Why can't my father look up with imagination?

I always tell my students that the Universe expanding is nothing to be afraid of. It means that we can see the secrets, the beginnings. There's a story there, I tell them, and it begins far away and ends here, with us.

I have been a bad daughter. It's so easy to be a bad daughter. You lose your grandmother's turquoise ring. Or you don't go to your cousin's wedding. Or you drink beer in front of your mother on Thanksgiving. Or you correct her grammar. Or you ignore your little sister's sickness.

To be a good daughter, you must eat your mother's cooking and ignore the long black hairs in the food. You must resist the instinct to gag. You must pick out the hair and never tell your mother that you found it. Tell her you love her food. *Can I have more?*

So easy to be a bad daughter. Fill up until your belly is ready to explode with the beginning of that story you're trying to tell.

My father's new love is American. She knows a lot of Persians, though, because she lives in Los Angeles. She claims to understand the culture. I don't understand the culture.

My father, I'm sure, fell in love with this woman's openness, something very different from my mother's culture, her secretive nature. Even as a child, I had to pry stories out of my mother. She viewed her homeland as a secret, not as something anyone else should understand. My mother's brown skin always gave her away. But to my mother, this reveal was only an illusion. Her insides were much darker and much more different.

The secrets, my father couldn't stand them. During one of our conversations, he said, "I know she has nothing to hide, but it's her own belief that she does. I'm not a foolish American."

My mother always wanted me to marry a nice Persian boy.

৵৶

When you go to the Mauna Kea Observatories, you must climb
a sacred mountain. They say gods used to live here. You must
observe rituals to respect the ancestors. You must do things
right, *pono* in Hawaiian. I don't know the word in Farsi.

Marjan's mouth and eyes are dry. Her hair never left her. She
has gained a lot of weight. I don't know why she started eating
again.

"I feel like him," my sister says, "like I've got nothing, though
I've spent my whole life building an altar."

"An altar to what?" I ask.

She has my mother's brown skin, and it shines against New
York's winter-scape. "To everything," she says, both of her arms
sweeping the view before us: Central Park, nothingness.

I put my arm around her, and she looks at me, confused. We
aren't used to touching each other. "I'm hungry," I say, and lead
her to a hot dog stand nearby.

We eat, for the sacrifice has already been made. The steam
from the hot dog stand blows directly into our faces, thawing
us. My sister asks me where we can find a goat, and we are okay.
Happy for the joke.

My sister cannot smile anymore. Her muscles are gone,
atrophied or just out of practice. She smiles with her eyes looking
up at the sky, her hair blowing in the wind, her arm around me
that firmly pulls me in like I am a child in need of warmth.

My father's new love is a dental hygienist. What is in peoples'
mouths? Nothing. No words. Everyone is silent. Speaking
English is like being mute. And I don't know Farsi. My father
says one language is as good as another.

My mother's surgeries have gone well, and her eyesight is much
improved. When I bring Marjan home, my mother can see her.

"I missed you," my mother says. And then she is crying, and

Marjan is the one to console her. My mother will waste her new eyes with this crying. Marjan is crying now, too.

Still, we will eat.

When my mother was pregnant with Marjan, birds came very close to her. One bird in particular, a redbird, kept watch over her.

Then, the weather got colder, and the crows came. My mother was sitting outside one day. The birds surrounded her, and she couldn't see any light or feel the wind anymore. Only a moment. She swears in that time the crows stole my sister's soul.

This was one of our nighttime stories, one of our fairy tales. Marjan loved the story. She always said, "No, Mother, they were bringing my soul to my body," and ran around pretending to be a demon.

Marjan leaves for college, having permission to begin in the spring session. She wants to major in astronomy, be just like me. All I can wonder is when she's coming home. I'm afraid we've lost her again. I understand what it means to leave home now.

I have decided to stay home because my mother's eyesight is failing again.

My mother and I make it through the mild winter.

In early spring, she and I are sitting outside on the deck. We suck the salt off pistachio shells, eat the nut, and then suck at our own teeth to make sure we've gotten all of the meat.

My mother looks closely at me. "I can see your freckles," she says. I think she's lying.

The university calls and asks me if I'll be back in the fall. I tell them the story about Alfraganus, the astronomer Dante used almost exclusively to structure *The Divine Comedy*. Dante hardly ever mentions Alfraganus, but without the astronomer, *The Divine Comedy* wouldn't exist. That is the story of Alfraganus.

I tell the university that I will tell my story. *The world isn't big enough yet. I can still see the stars, so far away. The eyes can hold it all in if the mouth cannot. This is love.*

The university fires me.

My father has stopped talking to me. He is going to get married again.

Who is my father? My father is not my father. He is not the boy who grew up near the water or the man who left us. He is like the stories he told us, a copy. He cannot live in the summer or the winter. He cannot understand the secrets.

My father is happy. My sister is happy. My mother is getting closer. My sister asks, "What were you doing while I was sick?" I will miss being atop the mountain looking up and up and up into the beginning of so many stars and galaxies. But mostly, I will miss the freedom and the brisk wind. I am not ready to die.

I want to tell you the story of my mother's death, but it begins with another story, a love story. Qays and Leyli were in love. Their parents forbade their love because Qays was too rich for Leyli. In his sadness, Qays set out into the desert surrounding his village. Out there, he starved himself until his mind fed him. He had visions—of a wedding and of a long and happy life with Leyli. Of a world without parents. His visions were white like the sun.

They found him out there in the wilderness, birds pecking at his eyes. He had died of thirst. When Leyli saw his body, she kneeled and kissed his bloody eyes. She told the village people that Qays had not died of thirst but of thirst for love. And *she* would have given it to him, she yelled at them. Then, Leyli took her father's sword and put it through her own eyes. The villagers believed her then, that Qays had gone crazy but also that his insanity had passed on to her. The villagers renamed Qays, gave him a title, Majnun, which means "crazy for love." They did not rename Leyli, though she had the sickness, because women were not given titles. But she had the sickness. She would have given it to him.

I want to tell you the story of my mother's death. It doesn't seem fair, though, to reveal all of her secrets. Crying doesn't heal the eyes and instead is how we lose everything.

I want to tell you the story of my mother's death, but the stars have disappeared. I never knew this was why I shouldn't wish on them. No, it's not my fault. My sister, the demon, ate the stars. If I rub her belly, she'll smile and give them back to me.

I want to tell you the story of my mother's death, but the rice is burning.

I want to tell you the story of my mother's death, but it begins with me pretending that my father is dead. He died violently. Tiresias predicted it, and in the end, we return to the garden. My mother wanders, staring at flowers instead of smelling them. She finds the proof of my hatred, blood on a stone. No apples. I'm not hungry.

I want to tell you the story of my mother's death, but she is not dead. You knew that already. She can see now, and I'm afraid she'll never die.

I want to tell you the story of my mother's death, but we will have to go home, to Nayriz.

In the hellish summer, the lake in the middle of many mountains dries up. The lake serves those who are lucky. Their luck is not drowning. Those who drown have some luck, too, though. They are shielded from the sun, and they are on the other side of the mirror.

My mother and I climb down so deep. We kneel on the lakebed in the middle of many mountains and let the silt run through our fingers. We pray for all of the things that have left us.

NAHAL SUZANNE JAMIR earned her PhD from Florida State University. Her work has been published in or is forthcoming in *The South Carolina Review*, *Jabberwock Review*, *Meridian*, *The Los Angeles Review*, *Crab Orchard Review*, *Carolina Quarterly*, *Ruminate Magazine*, and *Passages North*. She won First Prize in the 2012 William Van Dyke Short Story Prize, by *Ruminate Magazine*, for "Stories My Mother Told Me," Second Prize in the 2012 Press 53 Open Awards in Flash Fiction for "Foundling," and Third Place in the 2010 Glimmer Train Very Short Fiction Award for "In Perfect English."

Cover artist ALAN JUDGE is a London-born creative designer with an extensive portfolio of work in the digital and physical worlds using materials such as wood, metal, glass and ceramics. "I am always searching for the next level in my art," he says. "It is really the next level in myself. Image making is my home, my distraction, my being."

Capturing, creating and recreating the image is Alan's lifelong passion. He is forever collecting images physically and mentally. "Coming from the poorer part of (the then East) London, I grew to create interior designs and objects in some of the city's best houses including the making of sculptures, furniture and images for walls."

Alan's ability to interpret clients' wishes individually, to produce innovative designs combined with his broad knowledge of materials and innovative creative techniques, means his clients are delighted and their expectations regularly exceeded.

Alan welcomes new commissions, always listens, and is happy to discuss plans and ideas. You can find Alan via www.judgedesign.co.uk.

CPSIA information can be obtained at www.ICGtesting.com
Printed in the USA
LVOW04s1918250813

349506LV00004B/789/P